The Golden Lion of Granpère
Trollope, Anthony

Published: 1871
Cátegorie(s): Fiction

About Trollope:

Anthony Trollope's father, Thomas Anthony Trollope, worked as a barrister. Thomas Trollope, though a clever and well-educated man and a Fellow of New College, Oxford, failed at the bar due to his bad temper. In addition, his ventures into farming proved unprofitable and he lost an expected inheritance when an elderly uncle married and had children. Nonetheless, he came from a genteel background, with connections to the landed gentry, and so wished to educate his sons as gentlemen and for them to attend Oxford or Cambridge. The disparity between his family's social background and its poverty would be the cause of much misery to Anthony Trollope during his boyhood. Born in London, Anthony attended Harrow School as a day-boy for three years from the age of seven, as his father's farm lay in that neighbourhood. After a spell at a private school, he followed his father and two older brothers to Winchester College, where he remained for three years. He returned to Harrow as a day-boy to reduce the cost of his education. Trollope had some very miserable experiences at these two public schools. They ranked as two of the most élite schools in England, but Trollope had no money and no friends, and got bullied a great deal. At the age of twelve, he fantasized about suicide. However, he also daydreamed, constructing elaborate imaginary worlds. In 1827, his mother Frances Trollope moved to America with Trollope's three younger siblings, where she opened a bazaar in Cincinnati, which proved unsuccessful. Thomas Trollope joined them for a short time before returning to the farm at Harrow, but Anthony stayed in England throughout. His mother returned in 1831 and rapidly made a name for herself as a writer, soon earning a good income. His father's affairs, however, went from bad to worse. He gave up his legal practice entirely and failed to make enough income from farming to pay rents to his landlord Lord Northwick. In 1834 he fled to Belgium to avoid arrest for debt. The whole family moved to a house near Bruges, where they lived entirely on Frances's earnings. In 1835, Thomas Trollope died. While living in Belgium, Anthony worked as a Classics usher (a junior or assistant teacher) in a school with a view to learning French and German, so that he could take up a promised commission in an Austrian cavalry regiment, which had to be cut short at six weeks. He then obtained a position as a civil servant in the British Post Office through one of his mother's family connections, and returned to London on his own. This provided a respectable, gentlemanly occupation, but not a well-paid one. (from Wikipedia)

Also available for Trollope:
- *The Way We Live Now* (1875)
- *Barchester Towers* (1857)
- *The Warden* (1855)
- *The American Senator* (1877)
- *An Eye for an Eye* (1879)
- *Can You Forgive Her?* (1864)
- *Doctor Thorne* (1858)
- *Phineas Finn: The Irish Member* (1869)
- *The Last Chronicle of Barset* (1867)
- *The Small House at Allington* (1864)

Chapter 1

Up among the Vosges mountains in Lorraine, but just outside the old half-German province of Alsace, about thirty miles distant from the new and thoroughly French baths of Plombières, there lies the village of Granpere. Whatever may be said or thought here in England of the late imperial rule in France, it must at any rate be admitted that good roads were made under the Empire. Alsace, which twenty years ago seems to have been somewhat behindhand in this respect, received her full share of Napoleon's attention, and Granpere is now placed on an excellent road which runs from the town of Remiremont on one line of railway, to Colmar on another. The inhabitants of the Alsatian Ballon hills and the open valleys among them seem to think that the civilisation of great cities has been brought near enough to them, as there is already a diligence running daily from Granpere to Remiremont; - and at Remiremont you are on the railway, and, of course, in the middle of everything.

And indeed an observant traveller will be led to think that a great deal of what may most truly be called civilisation has found its way in among the Ballons, whether it travelled thither by the new-fangled railways and imperial routes, or found its passage along the valley streams before imperial favours had been showered upon the district. We are told that when Pastor Oberlin was appointed to his cure as Protestant clergyman in the Ban de la Roche a little more than one hundred years ago, - that was, in 1767, - this region was densely dark and far behind in the world's running as regards all progress. The people were ignorant, poor, half-starved, almost savage, destitute of communication, and unable to produce from their own soil enough food for their own sustenance. Of manufacturing enterprise they understood nothing, and were only just far enough advanced in knowledge for the Protestants to hate the Catholics, and the Catholics to hate the Protestants. Then came that wonderful clergyman, Pastor Oberlin, - he was indeed a wonderful clergyman, - and made a great change. Since that there have been the two empires, and Alsace has looked up in the world. Whether the thanks of the people are more honestly due to Oberlin or to the late Emperor, the author of this little story will not pretend to say; but he will venture to express his opinion that at present the rural Alsatians are a happy, prosperous people, with the burden on their shoulders of but few paupers, and fewer gentlemen, - apparently a contented people, not ambitious, given but little to politics. Protestants and Catholics mingled without hatred or fanaticism, educated though not learned, industrious though not energetic, quiet and peaceful, making linen and cheese, growing potatoes, importing corn, coming into the world, marrying, begetting children, and dying in the wholesome homespun fashion which is so sweet to us in that mood of philosophy which teaches us to love the country and to despise the town. Whether it be better for a people to achieve an even level of prosperity, which is shared by all, but which makes none eminent, or to encounter those rough, ambitious, competitive strengths which produce both palaces and poor-houses, shall not be matter of argument here; but the teller of this story is disposed to think that the chance traveller, as long as he tarries at Granpere, will insensibly and perhaps unconsciously become an advocate of the former doctrine; he will be struck by the comfort which he sees around him, and for a while will dispense with wealth, luxury, scholarships, and fashion. Whether the inhabitants of these hills and valleys will advance to farther progress now that they are again to become German, is another question, which the writer will not attempt to answer here.

Granpere in itself is a very pleasing village. Though the amount of population and number of houses do not suffice to make it more than a village, it covers so large a space of ground as almost to give it a claim to town honours. It is perhaps a full mile in length; and though it has but one street, there are buildings standing here and there, back from the line, which make it seem to stretch beyond the narrow confines of a single thoroughfare. In most French villages some of the houses are high and spacious, but here they seem almost all to be so. And many of them have been constructed after that independent fashion which always gives to a house in a street a character and importance of its own. They do not stand in a simple line, each supported by the strength of its neighbour, but occupy their own ground, facing this way or that as each may please, presenting here a corner to the main street, and there an end. There are little gardens, and big stables, and commodious barns; and periodical paint with annual white-wash is not wanting. The unstinted slates shine copiously under the sun, and over almost every other door there is a large lettered board which indicates that the resident within is a dealer in the linen which is produced throughout the country. All these things together give to Granpere an air of prosperity and comfort which is not at all checked by the fact that there is in the place no mansion which we Englishmen would call the gentleman's house, nothing approaching to the ascendancy of a parish squire, no baron's castle, no manorial hall, - not even a château to overshadow the modest roofs of the dealers in the linen of the Vosges.

And the scenery round Granpere is very pleasant, though the neighbouring hills never rise to the magnificence of mountains or produce that grandeur which tourists desire when they travel in search of the beauties of Nature. It is a spot to love if you know it well, rather than to visit with hopes raised high, and to leave with vivid impressions. There is water in abundance; a pretty lake lying at the feet of sloping hills, rivulets running down from the high upper lands and turning many a modest wheel in their course, a waterfall or two here and there, and a so-called mountain summit within an easy distance, from whence the sun may be seen to rise among the Swiss mountains; - and distant perhaps three miles from the village the main river which runs down the valley makes for itself a wild ravine, just where the bridge on the new road to Münster crosses the water, and helps to excuse the people of Granpere for claiming for themselves a great object of natural attraction. The bridge and the river and the ravine are very pretty, and perhaps justify all that the villagers say of them when they sing to travellers the praises of their country.

Whether it be the sale of linen that has produced the large inn at Granpere, or the delicious air of the place, or the ravine and the bridge, matters little to our story; but the fact of the inn matters very much. There it is, - a roomy, commodious building, not easily intelligible to a stranger, with its widely distributed parts, standing like an inverted V, with its open side towards the main road. On the ground-floor on one side are the large stables and coach-house, with a billiard-room and *café* over them, and a long balcony which runs round the building; and on the other side there are kitchens and drinking-rooms, and over these the chamber for meals and the bedrooms. All large, airy, and clean, though, perhaps, not excellently well finished in their construction, and furnished with but little pretence to French luxury. And behind the inn there are gardens, by no means trim, and a dusty summer-house, which serves, however, for the smoking of a cigar; and there is generally space and plenty and goodwill. Either the linen, or the air, or the ravine, or, as is more probable, the three combined, have produced a business, so that the landlord of the Lion d'Or at Granpere is a thriving man.

The reader shall at once be introduced to the landlord, and informed at the same time that, in so far as he may be interested in this story, he will have to take up his abode at the Lion d'Or till it be concluded; not as a guest staying loosely at his inn, but as one who is concerned with all the innermost affairs of the household. He will not simply eat his plate of soup, and drink his glass of wine, and pass on, knowing and caring more for the servant than for the servant's master, but he must content himself to sit at the landlord's table, to converse very frequently with the landlord's wife, to become very intimate with the landlord's son - whether on loving or on unloving terms shall be left entirely to himself - and to throw himself, with the sympathy of old friendship, into all the troubles and all the joys of the landlord's niece. If the reader be one who cannot take such a journey, and pass a month or two without the society of persons whom he would define as ladies and gentlemen, he had better be warned at once, and move on, not setting foot within the Lion d'Or at Granpere.

Michel Voss, the landlord, in person was at this time a tall, stout, active, and very handsome man, about fifty years of age. As his son was already twenty-five - and was known to be so throughout the commune - people were sure that Michel Voss was fifty or thereabouts; but there was very little in his appearance to indicate so many years. He was fat and burly to be sure; but then he was not fat to lethargy, or burly with any sign of slowness. There was still the spring of youth in his footstep, and when there was some weight to be lifted, some heavy timber to be thrust here or there, some huge lumbering vehicle to be hoisted in or out, there was no arm about the place so strong as that of the master. His short, dark, curly hair - that was always kept clipped round his head - was beginning to show a tinge of gray, but the huge moustache on his upper lip was still of a thorough brown, as was also the small morsel of beard which he wore upon his chin. He had bright sharp brown eyes, a nose slightly beaked, and a large mouth. He was on the whole a man of good temper, just withal, and one who loved those who belonged to him; but he chose to be master in his own house, and was apt to think that his superior years enabled him to know what younger people wanted better than they would know themselves. He was loved in his house and respected in his village; but there was something in the beak of his nose and the brightness of his eye which was apt to make those around him afraid of him. And indeed Michel Voss could lose his temper and become an angry man.

Our landlord had been twice married. By his first wife he had now living a single son, George Voss, who at the time of our tale had already reached his twenty-fifth year. George, however, did not at this time live under his father's roof, having taken service for a time with the landlady of another inn at Colmar. George Voss was known to be a clever young man; many in those parts declared that he was much more so than his father; and when he became clerk at the Poste in Colmar, and after a year or two had taken into his hands almost the entire management of that house - so that people began to say that old-fashioned and wretched as it was, money might still be made there - people began to say also that Michel Voss had been wrong to allow his son to leave Granpere. But in truth there had been a few words between the father and the son; and the two were so like each other that the father found it difficult to rule, and the son found it difficult to be ruled.

George Voss was very like his father, with this difference, as he was often told by the old folk about Granpere, that he would never fill his father's shoes. He was a smaller man, less tall by a couple of inches, less broad in proportion across the shoulders, whose arm would never be so strong, whose leg would never grace a tight stocking with so full a development. But he had the same eye, bright and brown and very quick, the same mouth, the same aquiline nose, the same broad forehead and well-shaped chin, and the same look in his face which made men know as by instinct that he would sooner command than obey. So there had come to be a few words, and George Voss had gone away to the house of a cousin of his mother's, and had taken to commanding there.

Not that there had been any quarrel between the father and the son; nor indeed that George was aware that he had been in the least disobedient to his parent. There was no recognised ambition for rule in the breasts of either of them. It was simply this, that their tempers were alike; and when on an occasion Michel told his son that he would not allow a certain piece of folly which the son was, as he thought, likely to commit, George declared that he would soon set that matter right by leaving Granpere. Accordingly he did leave Granpere, and became the right hand, and indeed the head, and backbone, and best leg of his old cousin Madame Faragon of the Poste at Colmar. Now the matter on which these few words occurred was a question of love - whether George Voss should fall in love with and marry his step-mother's niece Marie Bromar. But before anything farther can be said of these few words, Madame Voss and her niece must be introduced to the reader.

Madame Voss was nearly twenty years younger than her husband, and had now been a wife some five or six years. She had been brought from Epinal, where she had lived with a married sister, a widow, much older than herself - in parting from whom on her marriage there had been much tribulation. 'Should anything happen to Marie,' she had said to Michel Voss, before she gave him her troth, 'you will let Minnie Bromar come to me?' Michel Voss, who was then hotly in love with his hoped-for bride - hotly in love in spite of his four-and-forty years - gave the required promise. The said 'something' which had been suspected had happened. Madame Bromar had died, and Minnie Bromar her daughter - or Marie as she was always afterwards called - had at once been taken into the house at Granpere. Michel never thought twice about it when he was reminded of his promise. 'If I hadn't promised at all, she should come the same,' he said. 'The house is big enough for a dozen more yet.' In saying this he perhaps alluded to a little baby that then lay in a cradle in his wife's room, by means of which at that time Madame Voss was able to make her big husband do pretty nearly anything that she pleased. So Marie Bromar, then just fifteen years of age, was brought over from Epinal to Granpere, and the house certainly was not felt to be too small because she was there. Marie soon learned the ways and wishes of her burly, soft-hearted uncle; would fill his pipe for him, and hand him his soup, and bring his slippers, and put her soft arm round his neck, and became a favourite. She was only a child when she came, and Michel thought it was very pleasant; but in five years' time she was a woman, and Michel was forced to reflect that it would not be well that there should be another marriage and another family in the house while he was so young himself, - there was at this time a third baby in the cradle, - and then Marie Bromar had not a franc of *dot*. Marie was the sweetest eldest daughter in the world, but he could not think it right that his son should marry a wife before he had done a stroke for himself in the world. Prudence made it absolutely necessary that he should say a word to his son.

Madame Voss was certainly nearly twenty years younger than her husband, and yet the pair did not look to be ill-sorted. Michel was so handsome, strong, and hale; and Madame Voss, though she was a comely woman, - though when she was brought home a bride to Granpere the neighbours had all declared that she was very handsome, - carried with her a look of more years than she really possessed. She had borne many of a woman's cares, and had known much of woman's sorrows before she had become wife to Michel Voss; and then when the babes came, and she had settled down as mistress of that large household, and taught herself to regard George Voss and Marie Bromar almost as her own children, all idea that she was much younger than her husband departed from her. She was a woman who desired to excel her husband in nothing, - if only she might be considered to be in some things his equal. There was no feeling in the village that Michel Voss had brought home a young wife and had made a fool of himself. He was a man entitled to have a wife much younger than himself.

Madame Voss in those days always wore a white cap and a dark stuff gown, which was changed on Sundays for one of black silk, and brown mittens on her hands, and she went about the house in soft carpet shoes. She was a conscientious, useful, but not an enterprising woman; loving her husband much and fearing him somewhat; liking to have her own way in certain small matters, but willing to be led in other things so long as those were surrendered to her; careful with her children, the care of whom seemed to deprive her of the power of caring for the business of the inn; kind to her niece, good-humoured in her house, and satisfied with the world at large as long as she might always be allowed to entertain M. le Curé at dinner on Sundays. Michel Voss, Protestant though he was, had not the slightest objection to giving M. le Curé his Sunday dinner, on condition that M. le Curé on these occasions would confine his conversation to open subjects. M. le Curé was quite willing to eat his dinner and give no offence.

A word too must be said of Marie Bromar before we begin our story. Marie Bromar is the heroine of this little tale; and the reader must be made to have some idea of her as she would have appeared before him had he seen her standing near her uncle in the long room upstairs of the hotel at Granpere. Marie had been fifteen when she was brought from Epinal to Granpere, and had then been a child; but she had now reached her twentieth birthday, and was a woman. She was not above the middle height, and might seem to be less indeed in that house, because her aunt and her uncle were tall; but she was straight, well made, and very active. She was strong and liked to use her strength, and was very keen about all the work of the house. During the five years of her residence at Granpere she had thoroughly learned the mysteries of her uncle's trade. She knew good wine from bad by the perfume; she knew whether bread was the full weight by the touch; with a glance of her eye she could tell whether the cheese and butter were what they ought to be; in a matter of poultry no woman in all the commune could take her in; she was great in judging eggs; knew well the quality of linen; and was even able to calculate how long the hay should last, and what should be the consumption of corn in the stables. Michel Voss was well aware before Marie had been a year beneath his roof that she well earned the morsel she ate and the drop she drank; and when she had been there five years he was ready to swear that she was the cleverest girl in Lorraine or Alsace. And she was very pretty, with rich brown hair that would not allow itself to be brushed out of its crisp half-curls in front, and which she always wore cut short behind, curling round her straight, well-formed neck. Her eyes were gray, with a strong shade indeed of green, but were very bright and pleasant, full of intelligence, telling stories by their glances of her whole inward disposition, of her activity, quickness, and desire to have a hand in everything that was being done. Her father Jean Bromar had come from the same stock with Michel Voss, and she, too, had something of that aquiline nose which gave to the innkeeper and his son the look which made men dislike to contradict them. Her mouth was large, but her teeth were very white and perfect, and her smile was the sweetest thing that ever was seen. Marie Bromar was a pretty girl, and George Voss, had he lived so near to her and not have fallen in love with her, must have been cold indeed.

At the end of these five years Marie had become a woman, and was known by all around her to be a woman much stronger, both in person and in purpose, than her aunt; but she maintained, almost unconsciously, many of the ways in the house which she had assumed when she first entered it. Then she had always been on foot, to be everybody's messenger, - and so she was now. When her uncle and aunt were at their meals she was always up and about, - attending them, attending the public guests, attending the whole house. And it seemed as though she herself never sat down to eat or drink. Indeed, it was rare enough to find her seated at all. She would have a cup of coffee standing up at the little desk near the public window when she kept her books, or would take a morsel of meat as she helped to remove the dishes. She would stand sometimes for a minute leaning on the back of her uncle's chair as he sat at his supper, and would say, when he bade her to take her chair and eat with them, that she preferred picking and stealing. In all things she worshipped her uncle, observing his movements, caring for his wants, and carrying out his plans. She did not worship her aunt, but she so served Madame Voss that had she been withdrawn from the household

Madame Voss would have found herself altogether unable to provide for its wants. Thus Marie Bromar had become the guardian angel of the Lion d'Or at Granpere.

There must be a word or two more said of the difference between George Voss and his father which had ended in sending George to Colmar; a word or two about that, and a word also of what occurred between George and Marie. Then we shall be able to commence our story without farther reference to things past. As Michel Voss was a just, affectionate, and intelligent man, he would not probably have objected to a marriage between the two young people, had the proposition for such a marriage been first submitted to him, with a proper amount of attention to his judgment and controlling power. But the idea was introduced to him in a manner which taught him to think that there was to be a clandestine love affair. To him George was still a boy, and Marie not much more than a child, and - without much thinking - he felt that the thing was improper.

'I won't have it, George,' he had said.

'Won't have what, father?'

'Never mind. You know. If you can't get over it in any other way, you had better go away. You must do something for yourself before you can think of marrying.'

'I am not thinking of marrying.'

'Then what were you thinking of when I saw you with Marie? I won't have it for her sake, and I won't have it for mine, and I won't have it for your own. You had better go away for a while.'

'I'll go away to-morrow if you wish it, father.' Michel had turned away, not saying another word; and on the following day George did go away, hardly waiting an hour to set in order his part of his father's business. For it must be known that George had not been an idler in his father's establishment. There was a trade of wood-cutting upon the mountain-side, with a saw-mill turned by water beneath, over which George had presided almost since he had left the school of the commune. When his father told him that he was bound to do something before he got married, he could not have intended to accuse him of having been hitherto idle. Of the wood-cutting and the saw-mill George knew as much as Marie did of the poultry and the linen. Michel was wrong, probably, in his attempt to separate them. The house was large enough, or if not, there was still room for another house to be built in Granpere. They would have done well as man and wife. But then the head of a household naturally objects to seeing the boys and girls belonging to him making love under his nose without any reference to his opinion. 'Things were not made so easy for me,' he says to himself, and feels it to be a sort of duty to take care that the course of love shall not run altogether smooth. George, no doubt, was too abrupt with his father; or perhaps it might be the case that he was not sorry to take an opportunity of leaving for a while Granpere and Marie Bromar. It might be well to see the world; and though Marie Bromar was bright and pretty, it might be that there were others abroad brighter and prettier.

His father had spoken to him on one fine September afternoon, and within an hour George was with the men who were stripping bark from the great pine logs up on the side of the mountain. With them, and with two or three others who were engaged at the saw-mills, he remained till the night was dark. Then he came down and told something of his intentions to his stepmother. He was going to Colmar on the morrow with a horse and small cart, and would take with him what clothes he had ready. He did not speak to Marie that night, but he said something to his father about the timber and the mill. Gaspar Muntz, the head woodsman, knew, he said, all about the business. Gaspar could carry on the work till it would suit Michel Voss himself to see how things were going on. Michel Voss was sore and angry, but he said nothing. He sent to his son a couple of hundred francs by his wife, but said no word of explanation even to her. On the following morning George was off without seeing his father.

But Marie was up to give him his breakfast. 'What is the meaning of this, George?' she said.

'Father says that I shall be better away from this, - so I'm going away.'

'And why will you be better away?' To this George made no answer. 'It will be terrible if you quarrel with your father. Nothing can be so bad as that.'

'We have not quarrelled. That is to say, I have not quarrelled with him. If he quarrels with me, I cannot help it.'

'It must be helped,' said Marie, as she placed before him a mess of eggs which she had cooked for him with her own hands. 'I would sooner die than see anything wrong between you two.' Then there was a pause. 'Is it about me, George?' she asked boldly.

'Father thinks that I love you: - so I do.'

Marie paused for a few minutes before she said anything farther. She was standing very near to George, who was eating his breakfast heartily in spite of the interesting nature of the conversation. As she filled his cup a second time, she spoke again. 'I will never do anything, George, if I can help it, to displease my uncle.'

'But why should it displease him? He wants to have his own way in everything.'

'Of course he does.'

'He has told me to go; - and I'll go. I've worked for him as no other man would work, and have never said a word about a share in the business; - and never would.'

'Is it not all for yourself, George?'

'And why shouldn't you and I be married if we like it?'

'I will never like it,' said she solemnly, 'if uncle dislikes it.'

'Very well,' said George. 'There is the horse ready, and now I'm off.'

So he went, starting just as the day was dawning, and no one saw him on that morning except Marie Bromar. As soon as he was gone she went up to her little room, and sat herself down on her bedside. She knew that she loved him, and had been told that she was beloved. She knew that she could not lose him without suffering terribly; but now she almost feared that it would be necessary that she should lose him. His manner had not been tender to her. He had indeed said that he loved her, but there had been nothing of the tenderness of love in his mode of saying so; - and then he had said no word of persistency in the teeth of his father's objection. She had declared - thoroughly purposing that her declaration should be true - that she would never become his wife in opposition to her uncle's wishes; but he, had he been in earnest, might have said something of his readiness to attempt at least to overcome his father's objection. But he had said not a word, and Marie, as she sat upon her bed, made up her mind that it must be all over. But she made up her mind also that she would entertain no feeling of anger against her uncle. She owed him everything, so she thought - making no account, as George had done, of labour given in return. She was only a girl, and what was her labour? For a while she resolved that she would give a spoken assurance to her uncle that he need fear nothing from her. It was natural enough to her that her uncle should desire a better marriage for his son. But after a while she reflected that any speech from her on such a subject would be difficult, and that it would be better that she should hold her tongue. So she held her tongue, and thought of George, and suffered; - but still was merry, at least in manner, when her uncle spoke to her, and priced the poultry, and counted the linen, and made out the visitors' bills, as though nothing evil had come upon her. She was a gallant girl, and Michel Voss, though he could not speak of it, understood her gallantry and made notes of it on the note-book of his heart.

In the mean time George Voss was thriving at Colmar, - as the Vosses did thrive wherever they settled themselves. But he sent no word to his father, - nor did his father send word to him, - though they were not more than ten leagues apart. Once Madame Voss went over to see him, and brought back word of his well-doing.

Chapter 2

Exactly at eight o'clock every evening a loud bell was sounded in the hotel of the Lion d'Or at Granpere, and all within the house sat down together to supper. The supper was spread on a long table in the saloon up-stairs, and the room was lighted with camphine lamps, - for as yet gas had not found its way to Granpere. At this meal assembled not only the guests in the house and the members of the family of the landlord, - but also many persons living in the village whom it suited to take, at a certain price per month, the chief meal of the day, at the house of the innkeeper, instead of eating in their own houses a more costly, a less dainty, and probably a lonely supper. Therefore when the bell was heard there came together some dozen residents of Granpere, mostly young men engaged in the linen trade, from their different lodgings, and each took his accustomed seat down the sides of the long board, at which, tied in a knot, was placed his own napkin. At the top of the table was the place of Madame Voss, which she never failed to fill exactly three minutes after the bell had been rung. At her right hand was the chair of the master of the house, - never occupied by any one else; - but it would often happen that some business would keep him away. Since George had left him he had taken the timber into his own hands, and was accustomed to think and sometimes to say that the necessity was cruel on him. Below his chair and on the other side of Madame Voss there would generally be two or three places kept for guests who might be specially looked upon as the intimate friends of the mistress of the house; and at the farther end of the table, close to the window, was the space allotted to travellers. Here the napkins were not tied in knots, but were always clean. And, though the little plates of radishes, cakes, and dried fruits were continued from one of the tables to the other, the long-necked thin bottles of common wine came to an end before they reached the strangers' portion of the board; for it had been found that strangers would take at that hour either tea or a better kind of wine than that which Michel Voss gave to his accustomed guests without any special charge. When, however, the stranger should please to take the common wine, he was by no means thereby prejudiced in the eyes of Madame Voss or her husband. Michel Voss liked a profit, but he liked the habits of his country almost as well.

One evening in September, about twelve months after the departure of George, Madame Voss took her seat at the table, and the young men of the place who had been waiting round the door of the hotel for a few minutes, followed her into the room. And there was M. Goudin, the Curé, with another young clergyman, his friend. On Sundays the Curé always dined at the hotel at half-past twelve o'clock, as the friend of the family; but for his supper he paid, as did the other guests. I rather fancy that on week days he had no particular dinner; and indeed there was no such formal meal given in the house of Michel Voss on week days. There was something put on the table about noon in the little room between the kitchen and the public window; but except on Sundays it could hardly be called a dinner. On Sundays a real dinner was served in the room upstairs, with soup, and removes, and *entrées* and the *rôti,* all in the right place, - which showed that they knew what a dinner was at the Lion d'Or; - but, throughout the week, supper was the meal of the day. After M. Goudin, on this occasion, there came two maiden ladies from Epinal who were lodging at Granpere for change of air. They seated themselves near to Madame Voss, but still leaving a place or two vacant. And presently at the bottom of the table there came an Englishman and his wife, who were travelling through the country; and so the table was made up. A lad of about fifteen, who was known in Granpere as the waiter at the Lion d'Or, looked after the two strangers and the young men, and Marie Bromar, who herself had arranged the board, stood at the top of the room, by a second table, and dispensed the soup. It was pleasant to watch her eyes, as she marked the moment when the dispensing should begin, and counted her guests, thoughtful as to the sufficiency of the dishes to come; and noticed that Edmond Greisse had sat down with such dirty hands that she must bid her uncle to warn the lad; and observed that the more elderly of the two ladies from Epinal had bread too hard to suit her, - which should be changed as soon as the soup had been dispensed. She looked round, and even while dispensing saw everything. It was suggested in the last chapter that another house might have been built in Granpere, and that George Voss might have gone there, taking Marie as his bride; but the Lion d'Or would sorely have missed those quick and careful eyes.

Then, when that dispensing of the soup was concluded, Michel entered the room bringing with him a young man. The young man had evidently been expected; for, when he took the place close at the left hand of Madame Voss, she simply bowed to him, saying some word of courtesy as Michel took his place on the other side. Then Marie dispensed two more portions of soup, and leaving one on the farther table for the boy to serve, though she could well have brought the two, waited herself upon her uncle. 'And is Urmand to have no soup?' said Michel Voss, as he took his niece lovingly by the hand.

'Peter is bringing it,' said Marie. And in a moment or two Peter the waiter did bring the young man his soup.

'And will not Mademoiselle Marie sit down with us?' said the young man.

'If you can make her, you have more influence than I,' said Michel. 'Marie never sits, and never eats, and never drinks.' She was standing now close behind her uncle with both her hands upon his head; and she would often stand so after the supper was commenced, only moving to attend upon him, or to supplement the services of Peter and the maid-servant when she perceived that they were becoming for a time inadequate to their duties. She answered her uncle now by gently pulling his ears, but she said nothing.

'Sit down with us, Marie, to oblige me,' said Madame Voss.

'I had rather not, aunt. It is foolish to sit at supper and not eat. I have taken my supper already.' Then she moved away, and hovered round the two strangers at the end of the room. After supper Michel Voss and the young man - Adrian Urmand by name - lit their cigars and seated themselves on a bench outside the front door. 'Have you never said a word to her?' said Michel.

'Well; - a word; yes.'

'But you have not asked her - ; you know what I mean; - asked her whether she could love you.'

'Well, - yes. I have said as much as that, but I have never got an answer. And when I did ask her, she merely left me. She is not much given to talking.'

'She will not make the worse wife, my friend, because she is not much given to such talking as that. When she is out with me on a Sunday afternoon she has chat enough. By St. James, she'll talk for two hours without stopping when I'm so out of breath with the hill that I haven't a word.'

'I don't doubt she can talk.'

'That she can; and manage a house better than any girl I ever saw. You ask her aunt.'

'I know what her aunt thinks of her. Madame Voss says that neither you nor she can afford to part with her.'

Michel Voss was silent for a moment. It was dusk, and no one could see him as he brushed a tear from each eye with the back of his hand. 'I'll tell you what, Urmand, - it will break my heart to lose her. Do you see how she comes to me and comforts me? But if it broke my heart, and broke the house too, I would not keep her here. It isn't fit. If you like her, and she can like you, it will be a good match for her. You have my leave to ask her. She brought nothing here, but she has been a good girl, a very good girl, and she will not leave the house empty-handed.'

Adrian Urmand was a linen-buyer from Basle, and was known to have a good share in a good business. He was a handsome young man too, though rather small, and perhaps a little too apt to wear rings on his fingers and to show jewelry on his shirt-front and about his waistcoat. So at least said some of the young people of Granpere, where rings and gold studs are not so common as they are at Basle. But he was one who understood his business, and did not neglect it; he had money too; and was therefore such a young man that Michel Voss felt that he might give his niece to him without danger, if he and she could manage to like each other sufficiently. As to Urmand's liking, there was no doubt. Urmand was ready enough.

'I will see if she will speak to me just now,' said Urmand after a pause.

'Shall her aunt try it, or shall I do it?' said Michel.

But Adrian Urmand thought that part of the pleasure of love lay in the making of it himself. So he declined the innkeeper's offer, at any rate for the present occasion. 'Perhaps,' said he, 'Madame Voss will say a word for me after I have spoken for myself.'

'So let it be,' said the landlord. And then they finished their cigars in silence.

It was in vain that Adrian Urmand tried that night to obtain audience from Marie. Marie, as though she well knew what was wanted of her and was determined to thwart her lover, would not allow herself to be found alone for a moment. When Adrian presented himself at the window of her little bar, he found that Peter was with her, and she managed to keep Peter with her till Adrian was gone. And again, when he hoped to find her alone for a few moments after the work of the day was over in the small parlour where she was accustomed to sit for some half hour before she would go up to her room, he was again disappointed. She was already up-stairs with her aunt and the children, and all Michel Voss's good nature in keeping out of the way was of no avail.

But Urmand was determined not to be beaten. He intended to return to Basle on the next day but one, and desired to put this matter a little in forwardness before he took his departure. On the following morning he had various appointments to keep with countrymen and their wives, who sold linen to him, but he was quick over his business and managed to get back to the inn early in the afternoon. From six till eight he well knew that Marie would allow nothing to impede her in the grand work of preparing for supper; but at four o'clock she would certainly be sitting somewhere about the house with her needle in her hand. At four o'clock he found her, not with her needle in her hand, but, better still, perfectly idle. She was standing at an open window, looking out upon the garden as he came behind her, standing motionless with both hands on the sill of the window, thinking deeply of something that filled her mind. It might be that she was thinking of him.

'I have done with my customers now, and I shall be off to Basle to-morrow,' said he, as soon as she had looked round at the sound of his footsteps and perceived that he was close to her.

'I hope you have bought your goods well, M. Urmand.'

'Ah! for the matter of that the time for buying things well is clean gone. One used to be able to buy well; but there is not an old woman now in Alsace who doesn't know as well as I do, or better, what linen is worth in Berne and Paris. They expect to get nearly as much for it here at Granpere.'

'They work hard, M. Urmand, and things are dearer than they were. It is well that they should get a price for their labour.'

'A price, yes: - but how is a man to buy without a profit? They think that I come here for their sakes, - merely to bring the market to their doors.' Then he began to remember that he had no special object in discussing the circumstances of his trade with Marie Bromar, and that he had a special object in another direction. But how to turn the subject was now a difficulty.

'I am sure you do not buy without a profit,' said Marie Bromar, when she found that he was silent. 'And then the poor people, who have to pay so dear for everything!' She was making a violent attempt to keep him on the ground of his customers and his purchases.

'There was another thing that I wanted to say to you, Marie,' he began at last abruptly.

'Another thing,' said Marie, knowing that the hour had come.

'Yes; - another thing. I daresay you know what it is. I need not tell you now that I love you, need I, Marie? You know as well as I do what I think of you.'

'No, I don't,' said Marie, not intending to encourage him to tell her, but simply saying that which came easiest to her at the moment.

'I think this, - that if you will consent to be my wife, I shall be a very happy man. That is all. Everybody knows how pretty you are, and how good, and how clever; but I do not think that anybody loves you better than I do. Can you say that you will love me, Marie? Your uncle approves of it, - and your aunt.' He had now come quite close to her, and having placed his hand behind her back, was winding his arm round her waist.

'I will not have you do that, M. Urmand,' she said, escaping from his embrace.

'But that is no answer. Can you love me, Marie?'

'No,' she said, hardly whispering the word between her teeth.

'And is that to be all?'

'What more can I say?'

'But your uncle wishes it, and your aunt. Dear Marie, can you not try to love me?'

'I know they wish it. It is easy enough for a girl to see when such things are wished or when they are forbidden. Of course I know that uncle wishes it. And he is very good; - and so are you, I daresay. And I'm sure I ought to be very proud, because you are so much above me.'

'I am not a bit above you. If you knew what I think, you wouldn't say so.'

'But - '

'Well, Marie. Think a moment, dearest, before you give me an answer that shall make me either happy or miserable.'

'I have thought. I would almost burn myself in the fire, if uncle wished it.'

'And he does wish this.'

'But I cannot do this even because he wishes it.'

'Why not, Marie?'

'I prefer being as I am. I do not wish to leave the hotel, or to be married at all.'

'Nay, Marie, you will certainly be married some day.'

'No; there is no such certainty. Some girls never get married. I am of use here, and I am happy here.'

'Ah! it is because you cannot love me.'

'I don't suppose I shall ever love any one, not in that way. I must go away now, M. Urmand, because I am wanted below.'

She did go, and Adrian Urmand spoke no farther word of love to her on that occasion.

'I will speak to her about it myself,' said Michel Voss, when he heard his young friend's story that evening, seated again upon the bench outside the door, and smoking another cigar.

'It will be of no use,' said Adrian.

'One never knows,' said Michel. 'Young women are queer cattle to take to market. One can never be quite certain which way they want to go. After you are off to-morrow, I will have a few words with her. She does not quite understand as yet that she must make her hay while the sun shines. Some of 'em are

23

all in a hurry to get married, and some of 'em again are all for hanging back, when their friends wish it. It's natural, I believe, that they should be contrary. But Marie is as good as the best of them, and when I speak to her, she'll hear reason.'

Adrian Urmand had no alternative but to assent to the innkeeper's proposition. The idea of making love second-hand was not pleasant to him; but he could not hinder the uncle from speaking his mind to the niece. One little suggestion he did make before he took his departure. 'It can't be, I suppose, that there is any one else that she likes better?' To this Michel Voss made no answer in words, but shook his head in a fashion that made Adrian feel assured that there was no danger on that head.

But Michel Voss, though he had shaken his head in a manner so satisfactory, had feared that there was such danger. He had considered himself justified in shaking his head, but would not be so false as to give in words the assurance which Adrian had asked. That night he discussed the matter with his wife, declaring it as his purpose that Marie Bromar should marry Adrian Urmand. 'It is impossible that she should do better,' said Michel.

'It would be very well,' said Madame Voss.

'Very well! Why, he is worth thirty thousand francs, and is as steady at his business as his father was before him.'

'He is a dandy.'

'Psha! that is nothing!' said Michel.

'And he is too fond of money.'

'It is a fault on the right side,' said Michel. 'His wife and children will not come to want.'

Madame Voss paused a moment before she made her last and grand objection to the match. 'It is my belief,' said she, 'that Marie is always thinking of George.'

'Then she had better cease to think of him,' said Michel; 'for George is not thinking of her.' He said nothing farther, but resolved to speak his own mind freely to Marie Bromar.

Chapter 3

The old-fashioned inn at Colmar, at which George Voss was acting as assistant and chief manager to his father's distant cousin, Madame Faragon, was a house very different in all its belongings from the Lion d'Or at Granpere. It was very much larger, and had much higher pretensions. It assumed to itself the character of a first-class hotel; and when Colmar was without a railway, and was a great posting-station on the high road from Strasbourg to Lyons, there was some real business at the Hôtel de la Poste in that town. At present, though Colmar may probably have been benefited by the railway, the inn has faded, and is in its yellow leaf. Travellers who desire to see the statue which a grateful city has erected to the memory of its most illustrious citizen, General Rapp, are not sufficient in number to keep a first-class hotel in the glories of fresh paint and smart waiters; and when you have done with General Rapp, there is not much to interest you in Colmar. But there is the hotel; and poor fat, unwieldy Madame Faragon, though she grumbles much, and declares that there is not a sou to be made, still keeps it up, and bears with as much bravery as she can the buffets of a world which seems to her to be becoming less prosperous and less comfortable and more exacting every day. In her younger years, a posting-house in such a town was a posting-house; and when M. Faragon married her, the heiress of the then owner of the business, he was supposed to have done uncommonly well for himself. Madame Faragon is now a childless widow, and sometimes declares that she will shut the house up and have done with it. Why maintain a business without a profit, simply that there may be an Hôtel de la Poste at Colmar? But there are old servants whom she has not the heart to send away; and she has at any rate a roof of her own over her head; and though she herself is unconscious that it is so, she has many ties to the old business; and now, since her young cousin George Voss has been with her, things go a little better. She is not robbed so much, and the people of the town, finding that they can get a fair bottle of wine and a good supper, come to the inn; and at length an omnibus has been established, and there is a little glimmer of returning prosperity.

It is a large old rambling house, built round an irregularly-shaped court, with another court behind it; and in both courts the stables and coach-houses seem to be so mixed with the kitchens and entrances, that one hardly knows what part of the building is equine and what part human. Judging from the smell which pervades the lower quarters, and, alas, also too frequently the upper rooms, one would be inclined to say that the horses had the best of it. The defect had been pointed out to Madame Faragon more than once; but that lady, though in most of the affairs of life her temper is gentle and kindly, cannot hear with equanimity an insinuation that any portion of her house is either dirty or unsweet. Complaints have reached her that the beds were - well, inhabited - but no servant now dares to hint at anything wrong in this particular. If this traveller or that says a word to her personally in complaint, she looks as sour as death, and declines to open her mouth in reply; but when that traveller's back is turned, the things that Madame Faragon can say about the upstart coxcombry of the wretch, and as to the want of all real comforts which she is sure prevails in the home quarters of that ill-starred complaining traveller, are proof to those who hear them that the old landlady has not as yet lost all her energy. It need not be doubted that she herself religiously believes that no foul perfume has ever pervaded the sanctity of her chambers, and that no living thing has ever been seen inside the sheets of her beds, except those guests whom she has allocated to the different rooms.

Matters had not gone very easily with George Voss in all the changes he had made during the last year. Some things he was obliged to do without consulting Madame Faragon at all. Then she would discover what was going on, and there would be a 'few words.' At other times he would consult her, and carry his purpose only after much perseverance. Twice or thrice he had told her that he must go away, and then with many groans she had acceded to his propositions. It had been necessary to expend two thousand francs in establishing the omnibus, and in that affair the appearance of things had been at one time quite hopeless. And then when George had declared that the altered habits of the people required that the hour of the morning *table-d'hôte* should be changed from noon to one, she had sworn that she would not give way. She would never lend her assent to such vile idleness. It was already robbing the business portion of the day of an hour. She would wrap her colours round her and die upon the ground sooner than yield. 'Then they won't come,' said George, 'and it's no use you having the table then. They will all go to the Hôtel de l'Impératrice.' This was a new house, the very mention of which was a dagger-thrust into the bosom of Madame Faragon. 'Then they will be poisoned,' she said. 'And let them! It is what they are fit for.' But the change was made, and for the first three days she would not come out of her room. When the bell was rung at the obnoxious hour, she stopped her ears with her two hands.

But though there had been these contests, Madame Faragon had made more than one effort to induce George Voss to become her partner and successor in the house. If he would only bring in a small sum of money - a sum which must be easily within his father's reach - he should have half the business now, and all of it when Madame Faragon had gone to her rest. Or if he would prefer to give Madame Faragon a pension - a moderate pension - she would give up the house at once. At these tender moments she used to say that he probably would not begrudge her a room in which to die. But George Voss would always say that he had no money, that he could not ask his father for money, and that he had not made up his mind to settle at Colmar. Madame Faragon, who was naturally much interested in the matter, and was moreover not without curiosity, could never quite learn how matters stood at Granpere. A word or two she had heard in a circuitous way of Marie Bromar, but from George himself she could never learn anything of his affairs at home. She had asked him once or twice whether it would not be well that he should marry, but he had always replied that he did not think of such a thing - at any rate as yet. He was a steady young man, given more to work than to play, and apparently not inclined to amuse himself with the girls of the neighbourhood.

One day Edmond Greisse was over at Colmar - Edmond Greisse, the lad whose untidy appearance at the supper-table at the Lion d'Or had called down the rebuke of Marie Bromar. He had been sent over on some business by his employer, and had come to get his supper and bed at Madame Faragon's hotel. He was a modest, unassuming lad, and had been hardly more than a boy when George Voss had left Granpere. From time to time George had seen some friend from the village, and had thus heard tidings from home. Once, as has been said, Madame Voss had made a pilgrimage to Madame Faragon's establishment to visit him; but letters between the houses had not been frequent. Though postage in France - or shall we say Germany? - is now almost as low as in England, these people of Alsace have not yet fallen into the way of writing to each other when it occurs to any of them that a word may be said. Young Greisse had seen the landlady, who now never went upstairs among her guests, and had had his chamber allotted to him, and was seated at the supper-table, before he met George Voss. It was from Madame Faragon that George heard of his arrival.

'There is a neighbour of yours from Granpere in the house,' said she.

'From Granpere? And who is he?'

'I forget the lad's name; but he says that your father is well, and Madame Voss. He goes back early to-morrow with the roulage and some goods that his people have bought. I think he is at supper now.'

The place of honour at the top of the table at the Colmar inn was not in these days assumed by Madame Faragon. She had, alas, become too stout to do so with either grace or comfort, and always took her meals, as she always lived, in the little room downstairs, from which she could see, through the apertures of two doors, all who came in and all who went out by the chief entrance of the hotel. Nor had George usurped the place. It had now happened at Colmar, as it has come to pass at most hotels, that the public table is no longer the *table-d'hôte.* The end chair was occupied by a stout, dark man, with a bald head and black beard, who was proudly filling a place different from that of his neighbours, and who would probably have gone over to the Hôtel de l'Impératrice had anybody disturbed him. On the present occasion George seated himself next to the lad, and they were soon discussing all the news from Granpere.

'And how is Marie Bromar?' George asked at last.

'You have heard about her, of course,' said Edmond Greisse.

'Heard what?'

'She is going to be married.'

'Minnie Bromar to be married? And to whom?'

Edmond at once understood that his news was regarded as being important, and made the most of it.

'O dear, yes. It was settled last week when he was there.'

'But who is he?'

'Adrian Urmand, the linen-buyer from Basle.'

'Marie to be married to Adrian Urmand?'

Urmand's journeys to Granpere had been commenced before George Voss had left the place, and therefore the two young men had known each other.

'They say he's very rich,' said Edmond.

'I thought he cared for nobody but himself. And are you sure? Who told you?'

'I am quite sure; but I do not know who told me. They are all talking about it.'

'Did my father ever tell you?'

'No, he never told me.'

'Or Marie herself?'

'No, she did not tell me. Girls never tell those sort of things of themselves.'

'Nor Madame Voss?' asked George.

'She never talks much about anything. But you may be sure it's true. I'll tell you who told me first, and he is sure to know, because he lives in the house. It was Peter Veque.'

'Peter Veque, indeed! And who do you think would tell him?'

'But isn't it quite likely? She has grown to be such a beauty! Everybody gives it to her that she is the prettiest girl round Granpere. And why shouldn't he marry her? If I had a lot of money, I'd only look to get the prettiest girl I could find anywhere.'

After this, George said nothing farther to the young man as to the marriage. If it was talked about as Edmond said, it was probably true. And why should it not be true? Even though it were true, no one would have cared to tell him. She might have been married twice over, and no one in Granpere would have sent him word. So he declared to himself. And yet Marie Bromar had once sworn to him that she loved him, and would be his for ever and ever; and, though he had left her in dudgeon, with black looks, without a kind word of farewell, yet he had believed her. Through all his sojourn at Colmar he had told himself that she would be true to him. He believed it, though he was hardly sure of himself - had hardly resolved that he would ever go back to Granpere to seek her. His father had turned him out of the house, and Marie had told him as he went that she would never marry him if her uncle disapproved it. Slight as her word had been on that morning of his departure, it had rankled in his bosom, and made him angry with her through a whole twelvemonth. And yet he had believed that she would be true to him!

He went out in the evening when it was dusk and walked round and round the public garden of Colmar, thinking of the news which he had heard - the public garden, in which stands the statue of General Rapp. It was a terrible blow to him. Though he had remained a whole year in Colmar without seeing Marie, or hearing of her, without hardly ever having had her name upon his lips, without even having once assured himself during the whole time that the happiness of his life would depend on the girl's constancy to him, - now that he heard that she was to be married to another man, he was torn to pieces by anger and regret. He had sworn to love her, and had never even spoken a word of tenderness to another girl. She had given him her plighted troth, and now she was prepared to break it with the first man who asked her! As he thought of this, his brow became black with anger. But his regrets were as violent. What a fool he had been to leave her there, open to persuasion from any man who came in the way, open to persuasion from his father, who would, of course, be his enemy. How, indeed, could he expect that she should be true to him? The year had been long enough to him, but it must have been doubly long to her. He had expected that his father would send for him, would write to him, would at least transmit to him some word that would make him know that his presence was again desired at Granpere. But his father had been as proud as he was, and had not sent any such message. Or rather, perhaps, the father being older and less impatient, had thought that a temporary absence from Granpere might be good for his son.

It was late at night when George Voss went to bed, but he was up in the morning early to see Edmond Greisse before the roulage should start for Münster on its road to Granpere. Early times in that part of the world are very early, and the roulage was ready in the back court of the inn at half-past four in the morning.

'What? you up at this hour?' said Edmond.

'Why not? It is not every day we have a friend here from Granpere, so I thought I would see you off.'

'That is kind of you.'

'Give my love to them at the old house, Edmond.'

'Of course I will.'

'To father, and Madame Voss, and the children, and to Marie.'

'All right.'

'Tell Marie that you have told me of her marriage.'

'I don't know whether she'll like to talk about that to me.'

'Never mind; you tell her. She won't bite you. Tell her also that I shall be over at Granpere soon to see her and the rest of them. I'll be over - as soon as ever I can get away.'

'Shall I tell your father that?'

'No. Tell Marie, and let her tell my father.'

'And when will you come? We shall all be so glad to see you.'

'Never you mind that. You just give my message. Come in for a moment to the kitchen. There's a cup of coffee for you and a slice of ham. We are not going to let an old friend like you go away without breaking his fast.'

As Greisse had already paid his modest bill, amounting altogether to little more than three francs, this was kind of the young landlord, and while he was eating his bread and ham he promised faithfully that he would give the message just as George had given it to him.

It was on the third day after the departure of Edmond Greisse that George told Madame Faragon that he was going home.

'Going where, George?' said Madame Faragon, leaning forward on the table before her, and looking like a picture of despair.

'To Granpere, Madame Faragon.'

'To Granpere! and why? and when? and how? O dear! Why did you not tell me before, child?'

'I told you as soon as I knew.'

'But you are not going yet?'

'On Monday.'

'O dear! So soon as that! Lord bless me! We can't do anything before Monday. And when will you be back?'

'I cannot say with certainty. I shall not be long, I daresay.'

'And have they sent for you?'

'No, they have not sent for me, but I want to see them once again. And I must make up my mind what to do for the future.'

'Don't leave me, George; pray do not leave me!' exclaimed Madame Faragon. 'You shall have the business now if you choose to take it - only pray don't leave me!'

George explained that at any rate he would not desert her now at once; and on the Monday named he started for Granpere. He had not been very quick in his action, for a week had passed since he had given Edmond Greisse his breakfast in the hotel kitchen.

Chapter 4

Adrian Urmand had been three days gone from Granpere before Michel Voss found a fitting opportunity for talking to his niece. It was not a matter, as he thought, in which there was need for any great hurry, but there was need for much consideration. Once again he spoke on the subject to his wife.

'If she's thinking about George, she has kept it very much to herself,' he remarked.

'Girls do keep it to themselves,' said Madame Voss.

'I'm not so sure of that. They generally show it somehow. Marie never looks lovelorn. I don't believe a bit of it; and as for him, all the time he has been away he has never so much as sent a word of a message to one of us.'

'He sent his love to you, when I saw him, quite dutifully,' said Madame Voss.

'Why don't he come and see us if he cares for us? It isn't of him that Marie is thinking.'

'It isn't of anybody else then,' said Madame Voss. 'I never see her speak a word to any of the young men, nor one of them ever speaking a word to her.'

Pondering over all this, Michel Voss resolved that he would have it all out with his niece on the following Sunday.

On the Sunday he engaged Marie to start with him after dinner to the place on the hillside where they were cutting wood. It was a beautiful autumn afternoon, in that pleasantest of all months in the year, when the sun is not too hot, and the air is fresh and balmy, and one is still able to linger abroad, loitering either in or out of the shade, when the midges cease to bite, and the sun no longer scorches and glares; but the sweet vestiges of summer remain, and everything without doors is pleasant and friendly, and there is the gentle unrecognised regret for the departing year, the unconscious feeling that its glory is going from us, to add the inner charm of a soft melancholy to the outer luxury of the atmosphere. I doubt whether Michel Voss had ever realised the fact that September is the kindliest of all the months, but he felt it, and enjoyed the leisure of his Sunday afternoon when he could get his niece to take a stretch with him on the mountain-side. On these occasions Madame Voss was left at home with M. le Curé, who liked to linger over his little cup of coffee. Madame Voss, indeed, seldom cared to walk very far from the door of her own house; and on Sundays to go to the church and back again was certainly sufficient exercise.

Michel Voss said no word about Adrian Urmand as they were ascending the hill. He was too wise for that. He could not have given effect to his experience with sufficient eloquence had he attempted the task while the burden of the rising ground was upon his lungs and chest. They turned into a saw-mill as they went up, and counted the scantlings of timber that had been cut; and Michel looked at the cradle to see that it worked well, and to the wheels to see that they were in good order, and observed that the channel for the water required repairs, and said a word as to the injury that had come to him because George had left him. 'Perhaps he may come back soon,' said Marie. To this he made no answer, but continued his path up the mountain-side. 'There will be plenty of feed for the cows this autumn,' said Marie Bromar. 'That is a great comfort.'

'Plenty,' said Michel; 'plenty.' But Marie knew from the tone of his voice that he was not thinking about the grass, and so she held her peace. But the want or plenty of the pasture was generally a subject of the greatest interest to the people of Granpere at that special time of the year, and one on which Michel Voss was ever ready to speak. Marie therefore knew that there was something on her uncle's mind. Nevertheless he inspected the timber that was cut, and made some remarks about the work of the men. They were not so careful in barking the logs as they used to be, and upon the whole he thought that the wood itself was of a worse quality. What is there that we do not find to be deteriorating around us when we consider the things in detail, though we are willing enough to admit a general improvement? 'Yes,' said he, in answer to some remarks from Marie, 'we must take it, no doubt, as God gives it to us, but we need not spoil it in the handling. Sit down, my dear; I want to speak to you for a few minutes.' Then they sat down together on a large prostrate pine, which was being prepared to be sent down to the saw-mill. 'My dear,' said he, 'I want to speak to you about Adrian Urmand.' She blushed and trembled as she placed herself beside him; but he hardly noticed it. He was not quite at his ease himself, and was a little afraid of the task he had undertaken. 'Adrian tells me that he asked you to take him as your lover, and that you refused.'

'Yes, Uncle Michel.'

'But why, my dear? How are you to do better? Perhaps I, or your aunt, should have spoken to you first, and told you that we thought well of the match.'

'It wasn't that, uncle. I knew you thought well of it; or, at least, I believed that you did.'

'And what is your objection, Marie?'

'I don't object to M. Urmand, uncle; - at least, not particularly.'

'But he says you do object. You would not accept him when he offered himself.'

'No; I did not accept him.'

'But you will, my dear, - if he comes again?'

'No, uncle.'

'And why not? Is he not a good young man?'

'O, yes, - that is, I daresay.'

'And he has a good business. I do not know what more you could expect.'

'I expect nothing, uncle, - except not to go away from you.'

'Ah, - but you must go away from me. I should be very wrong, and so would your aunt, to let you remain here till you lose your good looks, and become an old woman on our hands. You are a pretty girl, Marie, and fit to be any man's wife, and you ought to take a husband. I am quite in earnest now, my dear; and I speak altogether for your own welfare.'

'I know you are in earnest, and I know that you speak for my welfare.'

'Well; - well; - what then? Of course, it is only reasonable that you should be married some day. Here is a young man in a better way of business than any man, old or young, that comes into Granpere. He has a house in Basle, and money to put in it whatever you want. And for the matter of that, Marie, my niece shall not go away from me empty-handed.'

She drew herself closer to him and took hold of his arm and pressed it, and looked up into his face.

'I brought nothing with me,' she said, 'and I want to take nothing away.'

'Is that it?' he said, speaking rapidly. 'Let me tell you then, my girl, that you shall have nothing but your earnings, - your fair earnings. Don't you take trouble about that. Urmand and I will settle that between us, and I will go bail there shall be no unpleasant words. As I said before, my girl sha'n't leave my house empty-handed; but, Lord bless you, he would only be too happy to take you in your petticoat, just as you are. I never saw a fellow more in love with a girl. Come, Marie, you need not mind saying the word to me, though you could not bring yourself to say it to him.'

'I can't say that word, uncle, either to you or to him.'

'And why the devil not?' said Michel Voss, who was beginning to be tired of being eloquent.

'I would rather stay at home with you and my aunt.'

'O, bother!'

'Some girls stay at home always. All girls do not get married. I don't want to be taken to Basle.'

'This is all nonsense,' said Michel, getting up. 'If you're a good girl, you will do as you are told.'

'It would not be good to be married to a man if I do not love him.'

'But why shouldn't you love him? He's just the man that all the girls always love. Why don't you love him?'

As Michel Voss asked this last question, there was a tone of anger in his voice. He had allowed his niece considerable liberty, and now she was unreasonable. Marie, who, in spite of her devotion to her uncle, was beginning to think that she was ill-used by this tone, made no reply. 'I hope you haven't been falling in love with any one else,' continued Michel.

'No,' said Marie, in a low whisper.

'I do hope you're not still thinking of George, who has left us without casting a thought upon you. I do hope that you are not such a fool as that.' Marie sat perfectly silent, not moving; but there was a frown on her brow and a look of sorrow mixed with anger on her face. But Michel Voss did not see her face. He looked straight before him as he spoke, and was flinging chips of wood to a distance in his energy. 'If it's that, Marie, I tell you you had better get quit of it at once. It can come to no good. Here is an excellent husband for you. Be a good girl, and say that you will accept him.'

'I should not be a good girl to accept a man whom I do not love.'

'Is it any thought about George that makes you say so, child?' Michel paused a moment for an answer. 'Tell me,' he continued, with almost angry energy, 'is it because of George that you refuse yourself to this young man?'

Marie paused again for a moment, and then she replied, 'No, it is not.'

'It is not?'

'No, uncle.'

'Then why will you not marry Adrian Urmand?'

'Because I do not care for him. Why won't you let me remain with you, uncle?'

She was very close to him now, and leaning against him; and her throat was half choked with sobs, and her eyes were full of tears. Michel Voss was a soft-hearted man, and inclined to be very soft of heart where Marie Bromar was concerned. On the other hand he was thoroughly convinced that it would be for his niece's benefit that she should marry this young trader; and he thought also that it was his duty as her uncle and guardian to be round with her, and make her understand, that as her friends wished it, and as the young trader himself wished it, it was her duty to do as she was desired. Another uncle and guardian in his place would hardly have consulted the girl at all. Between his desire to have his own way and reduce her to obedience, and the temptation to put his arm round her waist and kiss away her tears, he was uneasy and vacillating. She gently put her hand within his arm, and pressed it very close.

'Won't you let me remain with you, uncle? I love you and Aunt Josey' (Madame Voss was named Josephine, and was generally called Aunt Josey) 'and the children. I could not go away from the children. And I like the house. I am sure I am of use in the house.'

'Of course you are of use in the house. It is not that.'

'Why, then, should you want to send me away?'

'What nonsense you talk, Marie! Don't you know that a young woman like you ought to be married some day - that is if she can get a fitting man to take her? What would the neighbours say of me if we kept you at home to drudge for us, instead of settling you out in the world properly? You forget, Marie, that I have a duty to perform, and you should not make it so difficult.'

'But if I don't want to be settled?' said Marie. 'Who cares for the neighbours? If you and I understand each other, is not that enough?'

'I care for the neighbours,' said Michel Voss with energy.

'And must I marry a man I don't care a bit for, because of the neighbours, Uncle Michel?' asked Marie, with something approaching to indignation in her voice.

Michel Voss perceived that it was of no use for him to carry on the argument. He entertained a half-formed idea that he did not quite understand the objections so strongly urged by his niece; that there was something on her mind that she would not tell him, and that there might be cruelty in urging the matter upon her; but, in opposition to this, there was his assured conviction that it was his duty to provide well and comfortably for his niece, and that it was her duty to obey him in acceding to such provision as he might make. And then this marriage was undoubtedly a good marriage - a match that would make all the world declare how well Michel Voss had done for the girl whom he had taken under his protection. It was a marriage that he could not bear to see go out of the family. It was not probable that the young linen-merchant, who was so well to do in the world, and who, no doubt, might have his choice in larger places than Granpere - it was not probable, Michel thought, that he would put up with many refusals. The girl would lose her chance, unless he, by his firmness, could drive this folly out of her. And yet how could he be firm, when he was tempted to throw his great arms about her, and swear that she should eat of his bread and drink of his cup, and be unto him as a daughter, till the last day of their joint existence. When she crept so close to him and pressed his arm, he was almost overcome by the sweetness of her love and by the tenderness of his own heart.

'It seems to me that you don't understand,' he said at last. 'I didn't think that such a girl as you would be so silly.'

To this she made no reply; and then they began to walk down the hill together.

They had walked half way home, he stepping a little in advance, - because he was still angry with her, or angry rather with himself in that he could not bring himself to scold her properly, - and she following close behind his shoulder, when he stopped suddenly and asked her a question which came from the direction his thoughts were taking at the moment. 'You are sure,' he said, 'that you are not doing this because you expect George to come back to you?'

'Quite sure,' she said, bearing forward a moment, and answering him in a whisper when she spoke.

'By my word, then, I can't understand it. I can't indeed. Has Urmand done anything to offend you?'

'Nothing, uncle.'

'Nor said anything?'

'Not a word; uncle. I am not offended. Of course I am much obliged to him. Only I don't love him.'

'By my faith I don't understand it. I don't indeed. It is sheer nonsense, and you must get over it. I shouldn't be doing my duty if I didn't tell you that you must get over it. He will be here again in another ten days, and you must have thought better of it by that time. You must indeed, Marie.'

Then they walked down the hill in silence together, each thinking intently on the purpose of the other, but each altogether misunderstanding the other. Michel Voss was assured - as she had twice implied as much - that she was altogether indifferent to his son George. What he might have said or done had she declared her affection for her absent lover, he did not himself know. He had not questioned himself on that point. Though his wife had told him that Marie was ever thinking of George, he had not believed that it was so. He had no reason for disliking a marriage between his son and his wife's niece. When he had first thought that they were going to be lovers, under his nose, without his permission, - going to commence a new kind of life between themselves without so much as a word spoken to him or by him, - he had found himself compelled to interfere, compelled as a father and an uncle. That kind of thing could never be allowed to take place in a well-ordered house without the expressed sanction of the head of the household. He had interfered, - rather roughly; and his son had taken him at his word. He was sore now at his son's coldness to him, and was disposed to believe that his son cared not at all for any one at Granpere. His niece was almost as dear to him as his son, and much more dutiful. Therefore he would do the best he could for his niece. Marie's declaration that George was nothing to her, - that she did not think of him, - was in accordance with his own ideas. His wife had been wrong. His wife was usually wrong when any headwork was required. There could be no good reason why Marie Bromar should not marry Adrian Urmand.

But Marie, as she knew very well, had never declared that George Voss was nothing to her, - that he was forgotten, or that her heart was free. He had gone from her and had forgotten her. She was quite sure of that. And should she ever hear that he was married to some one else, - as it was probable that she would hear some day, - then she would be free again. Then she might take this man or that, if her friends wished it - and if she could bring herself to endure the proposed marriage. But at present her troth was plighted to George Voss; and where her troth was given, there was her heart also. She could understand that such a circumstance, affecting one of so little importance as herself, should be nothing to a man like her uncle; but it was everything to her. George had forgotten her, and she had wept sorely over his want of constancy. But though telling herself that this certainly was so, she had declared to herself that she would never be untrue till her want of truth had been put beyond the reach of doubt. Who does not know how hope remains, when reason has declared that there is no longer ground for hoping?

Such had been the state of her mind hitherto; but what would be the good of entertaining hope, even if there were ground for hoping, when, as was so evident, her uncle would never permit George and her to be man and wife? And did she not owe everything to her uncle? And was it not the duty of a girl to obey her guardian? Would not all the world be against her if she refused this man? Her mind was tormented by a thousand doubts, when her uncle said another word to her, just as they were entering the village.

'You will try and think better of it; - will you not, my dear?' She was silent. 'Come, Marie, you can say that you will try. Will you not try?'

'Yes, uncle, - I will try.'

Michel Voss went home in a good humour, for he felt that he had triumphed; and poor Marie returned broken-hearted, for she was aware that she had half-yielded. She knew that her uncle was triumphant.

Chapter 5

When Edmond Greisse was back at Granpere he well remembered his message, but he had some doubt as to the expediency of delivering it. He had to reflect in the first place whether he was quite sure that matters were arranged between Marie and Adrian Urmand. The story had been told to him as being certainly true by Peter the waiter. And he had discussed the matter with other young men, his associates in the place, among all of whom it was believed that Urmand was certainly about to carry away the young woman with whom they were all more or less in love. But when, on his return to Granpere, he had asked a few more questions, and had found that even Peter was now in doubt on a point as to which he had before been so sure, he began to think that there would be some difficulty in giving his message. He was not without some little fear of Marie, and hesitated to tell her that he had spread the report about her marriage. So he contented himself with simply announcing to her that George Voss intended to visit his old home.

'Does my uncle know?' Marie asked.

'No; - you are to tell him,' said Greisse.

'I am to tell him! Why should I tell him? You can tell him.'

'But George said that I was to let you know, and that you would tell your uncle.' This was quite unintelligible to Marie; but it was clear to her that she could make no such announcement, after the conversation which she had had with her uncle. It was quite out of the question that she should be the first to announce George's return, when she had been twice warned on that Sunday afternoon not to think of him. 'You had better let my uncle know yourself,' she said, as she walked away. But young Greisse, knowing that he was already in trouble, and feeling that he might very probably make it worse, held his peace. When therefore one morning George Voss showed himself at the door of the inn, neither his father nor Madame Voss expected him.

But his father was kind to him, and his mother-in-law hovered round him with demonstrations of love and gratitude, as though much were due to him for coming back at all. 'But you expected me,' said George.

'No, indeed,' said his father. 'We did not expect you now any more than on any other day since you left us.'

'I sent word by Edmond Greisse,' said George. Edmond was interrogated, and declared that he had forgotten to give the message. George was too clever to pursue the matter any farther, and when he first met Marie Bromar, there was not a word said between them beyond what might have been said between any young persons so related, after an absence of twelve months. George Voss was very careful to make no demonstration of affection for a girl who had forgotten him, and who was now, as he believed, betrothed to another man; and Marie was determined that certainly no sign of the old love should first be shown by her. He had come back, - perhaps just in time. He had returned just at the moment in which something must be decided. She had felt how much there was in the little word which she had spoken to her uncle. When a girl says that she will try to reconcile herself to a man's overtures, she has almost yielded. The word had escaped her without any such meaning on her part, - had been spoken because she had feared to continue to contradict her uncle in the full completeness of a positive refusal. She had regretted it as soon as it had been spoken, but she could not recall it. She had seen in her uncle's eye and had heard in the tone of his voice for how much that word had been taken; - but it had gone forth from her mouth, and she could not now rob it of its meaning. Adrian Urmand was to be back at Granpere in a few days - in ten days Michel Voss had said; and there were those ten days for her in which to resolve what she would do. Now, as though sent from heaven, George had returned, in this very interval of time. Might it not be that he would help her out of her difficulty? If he would only tell her to remain single for his sake, she would certainly turn her back upon her Swiss lover, let her uncle say what he might. She would make no engagement with

George unless with her uncle's sanction; but a word, a look of love, would fortify her against that other marriage.

George, she thought, had come back a man more to be worshipped than ever, as far as appearance went. What woman could doubt for a moment between two such men? Adrian Urmand was no doubt a pretty man, with black hair, of which he was very careful, with white hands, with bright small dark eyes which were very close together, with a thin regular nose, a small mouth, and a black moustache, which he was always pointing with his fingers. It was impossible to deny that he was good-looking after a fashion; but Marie despised him in her heart. She was almost bigger than he was, certainly stronger, and had no aptitude for the city niceness and *point-device* fastidiousness of such a lover. George Voss had come back, not taller than when he had left them, but broader in the shoulders, and more of a man. And then he had in his eye, and in his beaked nose, and his large mouth, and well-developed chin, that look of command, which was the peculiar character of his father's face, and which women, who judge of men by their feelings rather than their thoughts, always love to see. Marie, if she would consent to marry Adrian Urmand, might probably have her own way in the house in everything; whereas it was certain enough that George Voss, wherever he might be, would desire to have his way. But yet there needed not a moment, in Marie's estimation, to choose between the two. George Voss was a real man; whereas Adrian Urmand, tried by such a comparison, was in her estimation simply a rich trader in want of a wife.

In a day or two the fatted calf was killed, and all went happily between George and his father. They walked together up into the mountains, and looked after the wood-cutting, and discussed the prospects of the inn at Colmar. Michel was disposed to think that George had better remain at Colmar, and accept Madame Faragon's offer. 'If you think that the house is worth anything, I will give you a few thousand francs to set it in order; and then you had better agree to allow her so much a year for her life.' He probably felt himself to be nearly as young a man as his son; and then remember too that he had other sons coming up, who would be able to carry on the house at Granpere when he should be past his work. Michel was a loving, generous-hearted man, and all feeling of anger with his son was over before they had been together two days. 'You can't do better, George,' he said. 'You need not always stay away from us for twelve months, and I might take a turn over the mountain, and get a lesson as to how you do things at Colmar. If ten thousand francs will help you, you shall have them. Will that make things go straight with you?' George Voss thought the sum named would make things go very straight; but as the reader knows, he had another matter near to his heart. He thanked his father; but not in the joyous thoroughly contented tone that Michel had expected. 'Is there anything wrong about it?' Michel said in that sharp tone which he used when something had suddenly displeased him.

'There is nothing wrong; nothing wrong at all,' said George slowly. 'The money is much more than I could have expected. Indeed I did not expect any.'

'What is it then?'

'I was thinking of something else. Tell me, father; is it true that Marie is going to be married to Adrian Urmand?'

'What makes you ask?'

'I heard a report of it,' said George. 'Is it true?'

The father reflected a moment what answer he should give. It did not seem to him that George spoke of such a marriage as though the rumour of it had made him unhappy. The question had been asked almost with indifference. And then the young man's manner to Marie, and Marie's manner to him, during the last two days had made him certain that he had been right in supposing that they had both forgotten the little tenderness of a year ago. And Michel had thoroughly made up his mind that it would be well that Marie should marry Adrian. He believed that he had already vanquished Marie's scruples. She had promised 'to try and think better of it,' before George's return; and therefore was he not justified in regarding the matter as almost settled? 'I think that they will be married,' said he to his son.

'Then there is something in it?'

'O, yes; there is a great deal in it. Urmand is very eager for it, and has asked me and her aunt, and we have consented.'

'But has he asked her?'

'Yes; he has done that too,' said Michel.

'And what answer did he get?'

'Well; - I don't know that it would be fair to tell that. Marie is not a girl likely to jump into a man's arms at the first word. But I think there is no doubt that they will be betrothed before Sunday week. He is to be here again on Wednesday.'

'She likes him, then?'

'O, yes; of course she likes him.' Michel Voss had not intended to say a word that was false. He was anxious to do the best in his power for both his son and his niece. He thoroughly understood that it was his duty as a father and a guardian to start them well in the world, to do all that he could for their prosperity, to feed their wants with his money, as a pelican feeds her young with blood from her bosom. Had he known the hearts of each of them, could he have understood Marie's constancy, or the obstinate silent strength of his son's disposition, he would have let Adrian Urmand, with his business and his house at Basle, seek a wife in any other quarter where he listed, and would have joined together the hands of these two whom he loved, with a paternal blessing. But he did not understand. He thought that he saw everything when he saw nothing; - and now he was deceiving his son; for it was untrue that Marie had any such 'liking' for Adrian Urmand as that of which George had spoken.

'It is as good as settled, then?' said George, not showing by any tone of his voice the anxiety with which the question was asked.

'I think it is as good as settled,' Michel answered. Before they got back to the inn, George had thanked his father for his liberal offer, had declared that he would accede to Madame Faragon's proposition, and had made his father understand that he must return to Colmar on the next Monday, - two days before that on which Urmand was expected at Granpere.

The Monday came, and hitherto there had been no word of explanation between George and Marie. Every one in the house knew that he was about to return to Colmar, and every one in the house knew that he had been entirely reconciled to his father. Madame Voss had asked some question about him and Marie, and had been assured by her husband that there was nothing in that suspicion. 'I told you from the beginning,' said he, 'that there was nothing of that sort. I only wish that George would think of marrying some one, now that he is to have a large house of his own over his head.'

George had determined a dozen times that he would, and a dozen times that he would not, speak to Marie about her coming marriage, changing his mind as often as it was formed. Of what use was it to speak to her? he would say to himself. Then again he would resolve that he would scorch her false heart by one withering word before he went. Chance at last arranged it for him. Before he started he found himself alone with her for a moment, and it was almost impossible that he should not say something. Then he did speak.

'They tell me you are going to be married, Marie. I hope you will be happy and prosperous.'

'Who tells you so?'

'It is true at any rate, I suppose.'

'Not that I know of. If my uncle and aunt choose to dispose of me, I cannot help it.'

'It is well for girls to be disposed of sometimes. It saves them a world of trouble.'

'I don't know what you mean by that, George; - whether it is intended to be ill-natured.'

'No, indeed. Why should I be ill-natured to you? I heartily wish you to be well and happy. I daresay M. Urmand will make you a good husband. Good-bye, Marie. I shall be off in a few minutes. Will you not say farewell to me?'

'Farewell, George.'

'We used to be friends, Marie.'

'Yes; - we used to be friends.'

'And I have never forgotten the old days. I will not promise to come to your marriage, because it would not make either of us happy, but I shall wish you well. God bless you, Marie.' Then he put his arm round her and kissed her, as he might have done to a sister, - as it was natural that he should do to Marie Bromar, regarding her as a cousin. She did not speak a word more, and then he was gone!

She had been quite unable to tell him the truth. The manner in which he had first addressed her made it impossible for her to tell him that she was not engaged to marry Adrian Urmand, - that she was determined, if possible, to avoid the marriage, and that she had no love for Adrian Urmand. Had she done so, she would in so doing have asked him to come back to her. That she should do this was impossible. And yet as he left her, some suspicion of the truth, some half-formed idea of the real state of the man's mind in reference to her, flashed across her own. She seemed to feel that she was specially unfortunate, but she felt at the same time that there was no means within her reach of setting things right. And she was as convinced as ever she had been, that her uncle would never give his consent to a marriage between her and George Voss. As for George himself, he left her with an assured conviction that she was the promised bride of Adrian Urmand.

Chapter 6

The world seemed very hard to Marie Bromar when she was left alone. Though there were many who loved her, of whose real affection she had no doubt, there was no one to whom she could go for assistance. Her uncle in this matter was her enemy, and her aunt was completely under her uncle's guidance. Madame Voss spoke to her often in these days of the coming of Adrian Urmand, but the manner of her speaking was such that no comfort could be taken from it. Madame Voss would risk an opinion as to the room which the young man ought to occupy, and the manner in which he should be fed and entertained. For it was thoroughly understood that he was coming on this occasion as a lover and not as a trader, and that he was coming as the guest of Michel Voss, and not as a customer to the inn. 'I suppose he can take his supper like the other people,' Marie said to her aunt. And again, when the question of wine was mooted, she was almost saucy. 'If he's thirsty,' she said, 'what did for him last week, will do for him next week: and if he's not thirsty, he had better leave it alone.' But girls are always allowed to be saucy about their lovers, and Madame Voss did not count this for much.

Marie was always thinking of those last words which had been spoken between her and George, and of the kiss that he had given her. 'We used to be friends,' he had said, and then he had declared that he had never forgotten old days. Marie was quick, intelligent, and ready to perceive at half a glance, - to understand at half a word, as is the way with clever women. A thrill had gone through her as she heard the tone of the young man's voice, and she had half told herself all the truth. He had not quite ceased to think of her. Then he went, without saying the other one word that would have been needful, without even looking the truth into her face. He had gone, and had plainly given her to understand that he acceded to this marriage with Adrian Urmand. How was she to read it all? Was there more than one way in which a wounded woman, so sore at heart, could read it? He had told her that though he loved her still, it did not suit him to trouble himself with her as a wife; and that he would throw upon her head the guilt of having been false to their old vows. Though she loved him better than all the world, she despised him for his thoughtful treachery. In her eyes it was treachery. He must have known the truth. What right had he to suppose that she would be false to him, - he, who had never known her to lie to him? And was it not his business, as a man, to speak some word, to ask some question, by which, if he doubted, the truth might be made known to him? She, a woman, could ask no question. She could speak no word. She could not renew her assurances to him, till he should have asked her to renew them. He was either false, or a traitor, or a coward. She was very angry with him; - so angry that she was almost driven by her anger to throw herself into Adrian's arms. She was the more angry because she was full sure that he had not forgotten his old love, - that his heart was not altogether changed. Had it appeared to her that the sweet words of former days had vanished from his memory, though they had clung to hers, - that he had in truth learned to look upon his Granpere experiences as the simple doings of his boyhood, - her pride would have been hurt, but she would have been angry with herself rather than with him. But it had not been so. The respectful silence of his sojourn in the house had told her that it was not so. The tremor in his voice as he reminded her that they once had been friends had plainly told her that it was not so. He had acknowledged that they had been betrothed, and that the plight between them was still strong; but, wishing to be quit of it, he had thrown the burden of breaking it upon her.

She was very wretched, but she did not go about the house with downcast eyes or humble looks, or sit idle in a corner with her hands before her. She was quick and eager in the performance of her work, speaking sharply to those who came in contact with her. Peter Veque, her chief minister, had but a poor time of it in these days; and she spoke an angry word or two to Edmond Greisse. She had, in truth, spoken no words to Edmond Greisse that were not angry since that ill-starred communication of which he had only given her the half. To her aunt she was brusque, and almost ill-mannered.

'What is the matter with you, Marie?' Madame Voss said to her one morning, when she had been snubbed rather rudely by her niece. Marie in answer shook her head and shrugged her shoulders. 'If you cannot put on a better look before M. Urmand comes, I think he will hardly hold to his bargain,' said Madame Voss, who was angry.

'Who wants him to hold to his bargain?' said Marie sharply. Then feeling ill-inclined to discuss the matter with her aunt, she left the room. Madame Voss, who had been assured by her husband that Marie had no real objection to Adrian Urmand, did not understand it all.

'I am sure Marie is unhappy,' she said to her husband when he came in at noon that day.

'Yes,' said he. 'It seems strange, but it is so, I fancy, with the best of our young women. Her feeling of modesty - of bashfulness if you will - is outraged by being told that she is to admit this man as her lover. She won't make the worse wife on that account, when he gets her home.'

Madame Voss was not quite sure that her husband was right. She had not before observed young women to be made savage in their daily work by the outrage to their modesty of an acknowledged lover. But, as usual, she submitted to her husband. Had she not done so, there would have come that glance from the corner of his eye, and that curl in his lip, and that gentle breath from his nostril, which had become to her the expression of imperious marital authority. Nothing could be kinder, more truly affectionate, than was the heart of her husband towards her niece. Therefore Madame Voss yielded, and comforted herself by an assurance that as the best was being done for Marie, she need not subject herself to her husband's displeasure by contradiction or interference.

Michel Voss himself said little or nothing to his niece at this time. She had yielded to him, making him a promise that she would endeavour to accede to his wishes, and he felt that he was bound in honour not to trouble her farther, unless she should show herself to be disobedient when the moment of trial came. He was not himself at ease, he was not comfortable at heart, because he knew that Marie was avoiding him. Though she would still stand behind his chair at supper, - when for a moment she would be still, - she did not put her hands upon his head, nor did she speak to him more than the nature of her service required. Twice he tried to induce her to sit with them at table, as though to show that her position was altered now that she was about to become a bride; but he was altogether powerless to effect any such change as this. No words that could have been spoken would have induced Marie to seat herself at the table, so well did she understand all that such a change in her habits would have seemed to imply. There was now hardly one person in the supper-room of the hotel who did not instinctively understand the reason which made Michel Voss anxious that his niece should sit down, and that other reason which made her sternly refuse to comply with his request. So, day followed day, and there was but little said between the uncle and the niece, though heretofore - up to a time still within a fortnight of the present day - the whole business of the house had been managed by little whispered conferences between them. 'I think we'll do so and so, uncle;' or, 'Just you manage it yourself, Marie.' Such and such-like words had passed every morning and evening, with an understanding between them full and complete. Now each was afraid of the other, and everything was astray.

But Marie was still gentle with the children: when she could be with them for half an hour, she would sit with them on her lap, or clustering round, kissing them and saying soft words to them, - even softer in her affection than had been her wont. They understood as well as everybody else that something was wrong, - that there was to be some change as to Marie which perhaps would not be a change for the better; that there was cause for melancholy, for close kissing as though such kissing were in preparation for parting, and for soft strokings with their little hands as though Marie were to be pitied for that which was about to come upon her. 'Isn't somebody coming to take you away?' little Michel asked her, when they were quite alone. Marie had not known how to answer him. She had therefore embraced him closely, and a tear fell upon his face. 'Ah,' he said, 'I know somebody is coming to take you away. Will not papa help you?' She had not spoken; but for the moment she had taken courage, and had resolved that she would help herself.

At length the day was there on which Adrian Urmand was to come. It was his purpose to travel by Mulhouse and Remiremont, and Michel Voss drove over to the latter town to fetch him. It was felt by every one - it could not be but felt - that there was something special in his coming. His arrival now was not like the arrival of any one else. Marie, with all her resolution that it should be like usual arrivals at the inn, could not avoid the making of some difference herself. A better supper was prepared than usual; and, at the last moment, she herself assisted in preparing it. The young men clustered round the door of the hotel earlier than usual to welcome the new-comer. M. le Curé was there with a clean white collar, and with his best hat. Madame Voss had changed her gown, and appeared in her own little room before her husband returned almost in her Sunday apparel. She had said a doubtful word to Marie, suggesting a clean ribbon, or an altered frill. Marie had replied only by a look. She would not have changed a pin for Urmand's coming, had all Granpere come round her to tell her that it was needful. If the man wanted more to eat than was customary, let him have it. It was not for her to measure her uncle's hospitality. But her ribbons and her pins were her own.

The carriage was driving up to the door, and Michel with his young friend descended among the circle of expectant admirers. Urmand was rich, always well dressed, and now he was to be successful in love. He had about him a look as of a successful prosperous lover, as he jumped out of the little carriage with his portmanteau in his hand, and his greatcoat with its silk linings open at the breast. There was a consciousness in him and in every one there that he had not come now to buy linen. He made his way into the little room where Madame Voss was standing up, waiting for him, and was taken by the hand by her. Michel Voss soon followed them.

'And where is Marie?' Michel asked.

An answer came from some one that Marie was upstairs. Supper would soon be ready, and Marie was busy. Then Michel sent up an order by Peter that Marie should come down. But Marie did not come down. 'She had gone to her own room,' Peter said. Then there came a frown on Michel's brow. Marie had promised to try, and this was not trying. He said no more till they went up to supper. There was Marie standing as usual at the soup tureen. Urmand walked up to her, and they touched each other's hand; but Marie said never a word. The frown on Michel's brow was very black, but Marie went on dispensing her soup.

Chapter 7

Adrian Urmand, in spite of his white hands and his well-combed locks and the silk lining to his coat, had so much of the spirit of a man that he was minded to hold his head well up before the girl whom he wished to make his wife. Michel during that drive from Remiremont had told him that he might probably prevail. Michel had said a thousand things in favour of his niece and not a word to her prejudice; but he had so spoken, or had endeavoured so to speak, as to make Urmand understand that Marie could only be won with difficulty, and that she was perhaps unaccountably averse to the idea of matrimony. 'She is like a young filly, you know, that starts and plunges when she is touched,' he had said. 'You think there is nobody else?' Urmand had asked. Then Michel Voss had answered with confidence, 'I am sure there is nobody else.' Urmand had listened and said very little; but when at supper he saw that the uncle was ruffled in his temper and sat silent with a black brow, that Madame Voss was troubled in spirit, and that Marie dispensed her soup without vouchsafing a look to any one, he felt that it behoved him to do his best, and he did it. He talked freely to Madame Voss, telling her the news from Basle, - how at length he thought the French trade was reviving, and how all the Swiss authorities were still opposed to the German occupation of Alsace; and how flax was likely to be dearer than ever he had seen it; and how the travelling English were fewer this year than usual, to the great detriment of the innkeepers. Every now and then he would say a word to Marie herself, as she passed near him, speaking in a cheery tone and striving his best to dispel a black silence which on the present occasion would have been specially lugubrious. Upon the whole he did his work well, and Michel Voss was aware of it; but Marie Bromar entertained no gentle thought respecting him. He was not wanted there, and he ought not to have come. She had given him an answer, and he ought to have taken it. Nothing, she declared to herself, was meaner than a man who would go to a girl's parents or guardians for support, when the girl herself had told him that she wished to have nothing to do with him. Marie had promised that she would try, but every feeling of her heart was against the struggle.

After supper Michel with his young friend sat some time at the table, for the innkeeper had brought forth a bottle of his best Burgundy in honour of the occasion. When they had eaten their fruit, Madame Voss left the room, and Michel and Adrian were soon alone together. 'Say nothing to her till to-morrow,' said Michel in a low voice.

'I will not,' said Adrian. 'I do not wonder that she should be put out of face if she knows why I have come.'

'Of course she knows. Give her to-night and to-morrow, and we will see how it is to be.' At this time Marie was up-stairs with the children, resolute that nothing should induce her to go down till she should be sure that their visitor had gone to his chamber. There were many things about the house which it was her custom to see in their place before she went to her rest, and nobody should say that she neglected her work because of this dressed-up doll; but she would wait till she was sure of him, - till she was sure of her uncle also. In her present frame of mind she could not have spoken to the doll with ordinary courtesy. What she feared was, that her uncle should seek her up-stairs.

But Michel had some idea that her part in the play was not an easy one, and was minded to spare her for that night. But she had promised to try, and she must be reminded of her promise. Hitherto she certainly had not tried. Hitherto she had been ill-tempered, petulant, and almost rude. He would not see her himself this evening, but he would send a message to her by his wife. 'Tell her from me that I shall expect to see smiles on her face to-morrow,' said Michel Voss. And as he spoke there certainly were no smiles on his own.

'I suppose she is flurried,' said Madame Voss.

'Ah, flurried! That may do for to-night. I have been very good to her. Had she been my own, I could not have been kinder. I have loved her just as if she were my own. Of course I look now for the obedience of a child.'

'She does not mean to be undutiful, Michel.'

'I do not know about meaning. I like reality, and I will have it too. I consulted herself, and was more forbearing than most fathers would be. I talked to her about it, and she promised me that she would do her best to entertain the man. Now she receives him and me with an old frock and a sulky face. Who pays for her clothes? She has everything she wants, - just as a daughter, and she would not take the trouble to change her dress to grace my friend, - as you did, as any daughter would! I am angry with her.'

'Do not be angry with her. I think I can understand why she did not put on another frock.'

'So can I understand. I can understand well enough. I am not a fool. What is it she wants, I wonder? What is it she expects? Does she think some Count from Paris is to come and fetch her?'

'Nay, Michel, I think she expects nothing of that sort.'

'Then let her behave like any other young woman, and do as she is bid. He is not old or ugly, or a sot, or a gambler. Upon my word and honour I can't conceive what it is that she wants. I can't indeed.' It was perhaps the fault of Michel Voss that he could not understand that a young woman should live in the same house with him, and have a want which he did not conceive. Poor Marie! All that she wanted now, at this moment, was to be let alone!

Madame Voss, in obedience to her husband's commands, went up to Marie and found her sitting in the children's room, leaning with her head on her hand and her elbow on the table, while the children were asleep around her. She was waiting till the house should be quiet, so that she could go down and complete her work. 'O, is it you, Aunt Josey?' she said. 'I am waiting till uncle and M. Urmand are gone, that I may go down and put away the wine and the fruit.'

'Never mind that to-night, Marie.'

'O yes, I will go down presently. I should not be happy if the things were not put straight. Everything is about the house everywhere. We need not, I suppose, become like pigs because M. Urmand has come from Basle.'

'No; we need not be like pigs,' said Madame Voss. 'Come into my room a moment, Marie. I want to speak to you. Your uncle

57

won't be up yet.' Then she led the way, and Marie followed her. 'Your uncle is becoming angry, Marie, because - '

'Because why? Have I done anything to make him angry?'

'Why are you so cross to this young man?'

'I am not cross, Aunt Josey. I went on just the same as I always do. If Uncle Michel wants anything else, that is his fault; - not mine.'

'Of course you know what he wants, and I must say that you ought to obey him. You gave him a sort of a promise, and now he thinks that you are breaking it.'

'I gave him no promise,' said Marie stoutly.

'He says that you told him that you would at any rate be civil to M. Urmand.'

'And I have been civil,' said Marie.

'You did not speak to him.'

'I never do speak to anybody,' said Marie. 'I have got something to think of instead of talking to the people. How would the things go, if I took to talking to the people, and left everything to that little goose, Peter? Uncle Michel is unreasonable, - and unkind.'

'He means to do the best by you in his power. He wants to treat you just as though you were his daughter.'

'Then let him leave me alone. I don't want anything to be done. If I were his daughter he would not grudge me permission to stop at home in his house. I don't want anything else. I have never complained.'

'But, my dear, it is time that you should be settled in the world.'

'I am settled. I don't want any other settlement, - if they will only let me alone.'

'Marie,' said Madame Voss after a short pause, 'I sometimes think that you still have got George Voss in your head.'

'Is it that, Aunt Josey, that makes my uncle go on like this?' asked Marie.

'You do not answer me, child.'

'I do not know what answer you want. When George was here, I hardly spoke to him. If Uncle Michel is afraid of me, I will give him my solemn promise never to marry any one without his permission.'

'George Voss will never come back for you,' said Madame Voss.

'He will come when I ask him,' said Marie, flashing round upon her aunt with all the fire of her bright eyes. 'Does any one say that I have done anything to bring him to me? If so, it is false, whoever says it. I have done nothing. He has gone away, and let him stay. I shall not send for him. Uncle Michel need not be afraid of me, because of George.'

By this time Marie was speaking almost in a fury of passion, and her aunt was almost subdued by her. 'Nobody is afraid of you, Marie,' she said.

'Nobody need be. If they will let me alone, I will do no harm to any one.'

'But, Marie, you would wish to be married some day.'

'Why should I wish to be married? If I liked him, I would take him, but I don't. O, Aunt Josey, I thought you would be my friend!'

'I cannot be your friend, Marie, if you oppose your uncle. He has done everything for you, and he must know best what is good for you. There can be no reason against M. Urmand, and if you persist in being so unruly, he will only think that it is because you want George to come back for you.'

'I care nothing for George,' said Marie, as she left the room; 'nothing at all - nothing.'

About half-an-hour afterwards, listening at her own door, she heard the sound of her uncle's feet as he went to his room, and knew that the house was quiet. Then she crept forth, and went about her business. Nobody should say that she neglected anything because of this unhappiness. She brushed the crumbs from the long table, and smoothed the cloth for the next morning's breakfast; she put away bottles and dishes, and she locked up cupboards, and saw that the windows and the doors were fastened. Then she went down to her books in the little office below stairs. In the performance of her daily duty there were entries to be made and figures to be adjusted, which would have been done in the course of the evening, had it not been that she had been driven upstairs by fear of her lover and her uncle. But by the time that she took herself up to bed, nothing had been omitted. And after the book was closed she sat there, trying to resolve what she would do. Nothing had, perhaps, given her so sharp a pang as her aunt's assurance that George Voss would not come back to her, as her aunt's suspicion that she was looking for his return. It was not that she had been deserted, but that others should be able to taunt her with her desolation. She had never whispered the name of George to any one since he had left Granpere, and she thought that she might have been spared this indignity. 'If he fancies I want to interfere with him,' she said to herself, thinking of her uncle, and of her uncle's plans in reference to his son, 'he will find that he is mistaken.' Then it occurred to her that she would be driven to accept Adrian Urmand to prove that she was heart-whole in regard to George Voss.

She sat there, thinking of it till the night was half-spent, and when she crept up cold to bed, she had almost made up her mind that it would be best for her to do as her uncle wished. As for loving the man, that was out of the question. But then would it not be better to do without love altogether?

Chapter 8

'How is it to be?' said Michel to his niece the next morning. The question was asked downstairs in the little room, while Urmand was sitting at table in the chamber above waiting for the landlord. Michel Voss had begun to feel that his visitor would be very heavy on hand, having come there as a visitor and not as a man of business, unless he could be handed over to the woman-kind. But no such handing over would be possible, unless Marie would acquiesce. 'How is it to be?' Michel asked. He had so prepared himself that he was ready in accordance with a word or a look from his niece either to be very angry, thoroughly imperious, and resolute to have his way with the dependent girl, or else to be all smiles, and kindness, and confidence, and affection. There was nothing she should not have, if she would only be amenable to reason.

'How is what to be, Uncle Michel?' said Marie.

The landlord thought that he discovered an indication of concession in his niece's voice, and began immediately to adapt himself to the softer courses. 'Well, Marie, you know what it is we all wish. I hope you understand that we love you well, and think so much of you, that we would not intrust you to any one living, who did not bear a high character and seem to deserve you.' He was looking into Marie's face as he spoke, and saw that she was soft and thoughtful in her mood, not proud and scornful as she had been on the preceding evening. 'You have grown up here with us, Marie, till it has almost come upon us with surprise that you are a beautiful young woman, instead of a great straggling girl.'

'I wish I was a great straggling girl still.'

'Do not say that, my darling. We must all take the world as it is, you know. But here you are, and of course it is my duty and your aunt's duty - ' it was always a sign of high good humour on the part of Michel Voss, when he spoke of his wife as being anybody in the household - 'my duty and your aunt's duty to see and do the best for you.'

'You have always done the best for me in letting me be here.'

'Well, my dear, I hope so. You had to be here, and you fell into this way of life naturally. But sometimes, when I have seen you waiting on the people about the house, I've thought it wasn't quite right.'

'I think it was quite right. Peter couldn't do it all, and he'd be sure to make a mess of it.'

'We must have two Peters; that's all. But as I was saying, that kind of thing was natural enough before you were grown up, and had become - what shall I say? - such a handsome young woman.' Marie laughed, and turned up her nose and shook her head; but it may be presumed that she received some comfort from her uncle's compliments. 'And then I began to see, and your aunt began to see, that it wasn't right that you should spend your life handing soup to the young men here.'

'It is Peter who always hands the soup to the young men.'

'Well, well; but you are waiting upon them, and upon us.'

'I trust the day is never to come, uncle, when I'm to be ashamed of waiting upon you.' When he heard this, he put his arm round her and kissed her. Had he known at that moment what her feelings were in regard to his son, he would have recommended Adrian Urmand to go back to Basle. Had he known what were George's feelings, he would at once have sent for his son from Colmar.

'I hope you may give me my pipe and my cup of coffee when I'm such an old fellow that I can't get up to help myself. That's the sort of reward we look forward to from those we love and cherish. But, Marie, when we see you as you are now - your aunt and I - we feel that this kind of thing shouldn't go on. We want the world to know that you are a daughter to us, not a servant.'

'O, the world - the world, uncle! Why should we care for the world?'

'We must care, my dear. And you yourself, my dear - if this went on for a few years longer, you yourself would become very tired of it. It isn't what we should like for you, if you were our own daughter. Can't you understand that?'

'No, I can't.'

'Yes, my dear, yes. I'm sure you do. Very well. Then there comes this young man. I am not a bit surprised that he should fall in love with you - because I should do it myself if I were not your uncle.' Then she caressed his arm. How was she to keep herself from caressing him, when he spoke so sweetly to her? 'We were not a bit surprised when he came and told us how it was. Nobody could have behaved better. Everybody must admit that. He spoke of you to me and to your aunt as though you were the highest lady in the land.'

'I don't want any one to speak of me as though I were a high lady.'

'I mean in the way of respect, my dear. Every young woman must wish to be treated with respect by any young man who comes after her. Well; - he told us that it was the great wish of his life that you should be his wife. He's a man who has a right to look for a wife, because he can keep a wife. He has a house, and a business, and ready money.'

'What's all that, uncle?'

'Nothing; - nothing at all. No more than that,' - saying which Michel Voss threw his right hand and arm loosely abroad; - 'no more than that, if he were not himself well-behaved along with it. We want to see you married to him, - your aunt and I, - because we are sure that he will be a good husband to you.'

'But if I don't love him, Uncle Michel?'

'Ah, my dear; that's where I think it is that you are dreaming, and will go on dreaming till you've lost yourself, unless your aunt and I interfere to prevent it. Love is all very well. Of course you must love your husband. But it doesn't do for young women to let themselves be run away with by romantic ideas; - it doesn't, indeed, my dear. I've heard of young women who've fallen in love with statues and men in armour out of poetry, and grand fellows that they put into books, and there they've been waiting, waiting, waiting, till some man in armour should come for them. The man in armour doesn't come. But sometimes there comes somebody who looks like a man in armour, and that's the worst of all.'

'I don't want a man in armour, Uncle Michel.'

'No, I daresay not. But the truth is, you don't know what you want. The proper thing for a young woman is to get herself well settled, if she has the opportunity. There are people who think so much of money, that they'd give a child almost to anybody as long as he was rich. I shouldn't like to see you marry a man as old as myself.'

'I shouldn't care how old he was if I loved him.'

'Nor to a curmudgeon,' continued Michel, not caring to notice the interruption, 'nor to an ill-tempered fellow, or one who gambled, or one who would use bad words to you. But here is a young man who has no faults at all.'

'I hate people who have no faults,' said Marie.

'Now you must give him an answer to-day or to-morrow. You remember what you promised me when we were coming home the other day.' Marie remembered her promise very well, and thought that a great deal more had been made of it than justice would have permitted. 'I don't want to hurry you at all, only it makes me so sad at heart when my own girl won't come and say a kind word to me and give me a kiss before we part at night. I thought so much of that last night, Marie, I couldn't sleep for thinking of it.' On hearing this, she flung her arms round his neck and kissed him on each cheek and on his lips. 'I get to feel so, Marie, if there's anything wrong between you and me, that I don't know what I'm doing. Will you do this for me, my dear? Come and sit at table with us this evening, and make one of us. At any rate, come and show that we don't want to make a servant of you. Then we'll put off the rest of it till to-morrow.' When such a request was made to her in such words, how could she not accede to it? She had no alternative but to say that she would do in this respect as he would have her. She smiled, and nodded her head, and kissed him again. 'And, Marie darling, put on a pretty frock, - for my sake. I like to see you gay and pretty.' Again she nodded her head, and again she kissed him. Such requests, so made, she felt that it would be impossible she should refuse.

And yet when she came to think of it as she went about the house alone, the granting of such requests was in fact yielding in everything. If she made herself smart for this young man, and sat next him, and smiled, and talked to him, conscious as she would be - and he would be also - that she was so placed that she might become his wife, how afterwards could she hold her ground? And if she were really resolute to hold her ground, would it not be much better that she should do so by giving up no point, even though her uncle's anger should rise hot against her? But now she had promised her uncle, and she knew that she could not go back from her word. It would be better for her, she told herself, to think no more about it. Things must arrange themselves. What did it matter whether she were wretched at Basle or wretched at Granpere? The only thing that could give a charm to her life was altogether out of her reach.

After this conversation, Michel went upstairs to his young friend, and within a quarter of an hour had handed him over to his wife. It was of course understood now that Marie was not to be troubled till the time came for her to sit down at table with her smart frock. Michel explained to his wife the full amount of his success, and acknowledged that he felt that Marie was already pretty nearly overcome.

'She'll try to be pleasant for my sake this evening,' he said, 'and so she'll fall into the way of being intimate with him; and when he asks her to-morrow she'll be forced to take him.'

It never occurred to him, as he said this, that he was forming a plan for sacrificing the girl he loved. He imagined that he was doing his duty by his niece thoroughly, and was rather proud of his own generosity. In the afternoon Adrian Urmand was taken out for a drive to the ravine by Madame Voss. They both, no doubt, felt that this was very tedious; but they were by nature patient - quite unlike Michel Voss or Marie - and each of them was aware that there was a duty to be done. Adrian therefore was satisfied to potter about the ravine, and Madame Voss assured him at least a dozen times that it was the dearest wish of her heart to call him her nephew-in-law.

At last the time for supper came. Throughout the day Marie had said very little to any one after leaving her uncle. Ideas flitted across her mind of various modes of escape. What if she were to run away - to her cousin's house at Epinal; and write from thence to say that this proposed marriage was impossible? But her cousin at Epinal was a stranger to her, and her uncle had always been to her the same as a father. Then she thought of going to Colmar, of telling the whole truth to George, and of dying when he refused her - as refuse her he would. But this was a dream rather than a plan. Or how would it be if she went to her uncle now at once, while the young man was away at the ravine, and swore to him that nothing on earth should induce her to marry Adrian Urmand? But brave as Marie was, she was afraid to do this. He had told her how he suffered when they two did not stand well together, and she feared to be accused by him of unkindness and ingratitude. And how would it be with her if she did accept the man? She was sufficiently alive to the necessities of the world to know that it would be well to have a home of her own, and a husband, and children if God would send them. She understood quite as well as Michel Voss did that to be head-waiter at the Lion d'Or was not a career in life of which she could have reason to be proud. As the afternoon went on she was in great doubt. She spread the cloth, and prepared the room for supper, somewhat earlier than usual, knowing that she should require some minutes for her toilet. It was necessary that she should explain to Peter that he must take upon himself some self-action upon this occasion, and it may be doubted whether she did this with perfect good humour. She was angry when she had to look for him before she commenced her operations, and scolded him because he could not understand without being told why she went away and left him twenty minutes before the bell was rung.

As soon as the bell was heard through the house, Michel Voss, who was waiting below with his wife in a quiet unusual manner, marshalled the way upstairs. He had partly expected that Marie would join them below, and was becoming fidgety lest she should break away from her engagement. He went first, and then followed Adrian and Madame Voss together. The accustomed guests were all ready, because it had come to be generally understood that this supper was to be as it were a supper of betrothal. Madame Voss had on her black silk gown. Michel had changed his coat and his cravat. Adrian Urmand was exceedingly smart. The dullest intellect could perceive that there was something special in the wind. The two old ladies who were lodgers in the house came out from their rooms five minutes earlier than usual, and met the *cortége* from downstairs in the passage.

When Michel entered the room he at once looked round for Marie. There she was standing at the soup-tureen with her back to the company. But he could see that there hung down some ribbon from her waist, that her frock was not the one she had worn in the morning, and that in the article of her attire she had kept her word with him. He was very awkward. When one of the old ladies was about to seat herself in the chair next to Adrian - in preparation for which it must be admitted that Marie had made certain wicked arrangements - Michel first by signs and afterwards with audible words, intended to be whispered, indicated to the lady that she was required to place herself elsewhere. This was hard upon the lady, as her own table-napkin and a cup out of which she was wont to drink were placed at that spot. Marie, standing at the soup-tureen, heard it all and became very spiteful. Then her uncle called to her:

'Marie, my dear, are you not coming?'

'Presently, uncle,' replied Marie, in a clear voice, as she commenced to dispense the soup.

She ladled out all the soup without once turning her face towards the company, then stood for a few moments as if in doubt, and after that walked boldly up to her place. She had intended to sit next to her uncle, opposite to her lover, and there had been her chair. But Michel had insisted on bringing the old lady round to the seat that Marie had intended for herself, and so had disarranged all her plans. The old lady had simpered and smiled and made a little speech to M. Urmand, which everybody had heard. Marie, too, had heard it all. But the thing had to be done, and she plucked up her courage and did it. She placed herself next to her lover, and as she did so, felt that it was necessary that she should say something at the moment:

'Here I am, Uncle Michel; but you'll find you'll miss me, before supper is over.'

'There is somebody would much rather have you than his supper,' said the horrid old lady opposite.

Then there was a pause, a terrible pause.

'Perhaps it used to be so when young men came to sup with you, years ago; but nowadays men like their supper,' said Marie, who was driven on by her anger to a ferocity which she could not restrain.

'I did not mean to give offence,' said the poor old lady meekly.

Marie, as she thought of what she had said, repented so bitterly that she could hardly refrain from tears.

'There is no offence at all,' said Michel angrily.

'Will you allow me to give you a little wine?' said Adrian, turning to his neighbour.

Marie bowed her head, and held her glass, but the wine remained in it to the end of the supper, and there it was left.

When it was all over, Michel felt that it had not been a success. With the exception of her savage speech to the disagreeable old lady, Marie had behaved well. She was on her mettle, and very anxious to show that she could sit at table with Adrian Urmand, and be at her ease. She was not at her ease, but she made a bold fight - which was more than was done by her uncle or her aunt. Michel was unable to speak in his ordinary voice or with his usual authority, and Madame Voss hardly uttered a word. Urmand, whose position was the hardest of all, struggled gallantly, but was quite unable to keep up any continued conversation. The old lady had been thoroughly silenced, and neither she nor her sister again opened their mouth. When Madame Voss rose from her chair in order that they might all retire, the consciousness of relief was very great.

For that night Marie's duty to her uncle was done. So much had been understood. She was to dress herself and sit down to supper, and after that she was not to be disturbed again till the morrow. On the next morning she was to be subjected to the grand trial. She understood this so well that she went about the house fearless on that evening - fearless as regarded the moment, fearful only as regarded the morrow.

'May I ask one question, dear?' said her aunt, coming to her after she had gone to her own room. 'Have you made up your mind?'

'No,' said Marie; 'I have not made up my mind.'

Her aunt stood for a moment looking at her, and then crept out of the room.

In the morning Michel Voss was half-inclined to release his niece, and to tell Urmand that he had better go back to Basle. He could see that the girl was suffering, and, after all, what was it that he wanted? Only that she should be prosperous and happy. His heart almost relented; and at one moment, had

Marie come across him, he would have released her. 'Let it go on,' he said to himself, as he took up his cap and stick, and went off to the woods. 'Let it go on. If she finds to-day that she can't take him, I'll never say another word to press her.' He went up to the woods after breakfast, and did not come back till the evening.

During breakfast Marie did not show herself at all, but remained with the children. It was not expected that she should show herself. At about noon, as soon as her uncle had started, her aunt came to her and asked her whether she was ready to see M. Urmand. 'I am ready,' said Marie, rising from her seat, and standing upright before her aunt.

'And where will you see him, dear?'

'Wherever he pleases,' said Marie, with something that was again almost savage in her voice.

'Shall he come up-stairs to you?'

'What, here?'

'No; he cannot come here. You might go into the little sitting-room.'

'Very well. I will go into the little sitting room.' Then without saying another word she got up, left the room, and went along the passage to the chamber in question. It was a small room, furnished, as they all thought at Granpere, with Parisian elegance, intended for such visitors to the hotel as might choose to pay for the charm and luxury of such an apartment. It was generally found that visitors to Granpere did not care to pay for the luxury of this Parisian elegance, and the room was almost always empty. Thither Marie went, and seated herself at once on the centre of the red, stuffy, velvet sofa. There she sat, perfectly motionless, till there came a knock at the door. Marie Bromar was a very handsome girl, but as she sat there, all alone, with her hands crossed on her lap, with a hard look about her mouth, with a frown on her brow, and scorn and disdain for all around her in her eyes, she was as little handsome as it was possible that she should make herself. She answered the knock, and Adrian Urmand entered the room. She did not rise, but waited till he had come close up to her. Then she was the first to speak. 'Aunt Josey tells me that you want to see me,' she said.

Urmand's task was certainly not a pleasant one. Though his temper was excellent, he was already beginning to think that he was being ill-used. Marie, no doubt, was a very fine girl, but the match that he offered her was one at which no young woman of her rank in all Lorraine or Alsace need have turned up her nose. He had been invited over to Granpere specially that he might spend his time in making love, and he had found the task before him very hard and disagreeable. He was afflicted with all the ponderous notoriety of an acknowledged suitor's position, but was consoled with none of the usual comforts. Had he not been pledged to make the attempt, he would probably have gone back to Basle; as it was, he was compelled to renew his offer. He was aware that he could not leave the house without doing so. But he was determined that one more refusal should be the last.

'Marie,' said he, putting out his hand to her, 'doubtless you know what it is that I would say.'

'I suppose I do,' she answered.

'I hope you do not doubt my true affection for you.'

She paused a moment before she replied. 'I have no reason to doubt it,' she said.

'No indeed. I love you with all my heart. I do truly. Your uncle and aunt think it would be a good thing for both of us that we should be married. What answer will you make me, Marie?' Again she paused. She had allowed him to take her hand, and as he thus asked his question he was standing opposite to her, still holding it. 'You have thought about it, Marie, since I was here last?'

'Yes; I have thought about it.'

'Well, dearest?'

'I suppose it had better be so,' said she, standing up and withdrawing her hand.

She had accepted him; and now it was no longer possible for him to go back to Basle except as a betrothed man. She had accepted him; but there came upon him a wretched feeling that none of the triumph of successful love had come to him. He was almost disappointed, - or if not disappointed, was at any rate embarrassed. But it was necessary that he should immediately conduct himself as an engaged man. 'And you will love me, Marie?' he said, as he again took her by the hand.

'I will do my best,' she said.

Then he put his arm round her waist and kissed her, and she did not turn away her face from him. 'I will do my best also to make you happy,' he said.

'I am sure you will. I believe you. I know that you are good.' There was another pause during which he stood, still embracing her. 'I may go now; may I not?' she said.

'You have not kissed me yet, Marie?' Then she kissed him; but the touch of her lips was cold, and he felt that there was no love in them. He knew, though he could hardly define the knowledge to himself, that she had accepted him in obedience to her uncle. He was almost angry, but being cautious and even-tempered by nature he repressed the feeling. He knew that he must take her now, and that he had better make the best of it. She would, he was sure, be a good wife, and the love would probably come in time.

'We shall be together this evening; shall we not?' he asked.

'O, yes,' said Marie, 'if you please.' It was, as she knew, only reasonable now that they should be together. Then he let her go, and she walked off to her room.

Chapter 9

'I suppose it had better be so,' Marie Bromar had said to her lover, when in set form he made his proposition. She had thought very much about it, and had come exactly to that state of mind. She did suppose that it had better be so. She knew that she did not love the man. She knew also that she loved another man. She did not even think that she should ever learn to love Adrian Urmand. She had neither ambition in the matter, nor even any feeling of prudence as regarded herself. She was enticed by no desire of position, or love of money. In respect to all her own feelings about herself she would sooner have remained at the Lion d'Or, and have waited upon the guests day after day, and month after month. But yet she had supposed 'that it had better be so.' Her uncle wished it, - wished it so strongly that she believed it would be impossible that she could remain an inmate in his house, unless she acceded to his wishes. Her aunt manifestly thought that it was her duty to accept the man, and could not understand how so manifest a duty, going hand in hand as it did with so great an advantage, should be made a matter of doubt. She had not one about her to counsel her to hold by her own feelings. It was the practice of the world around her that girls in such matters should do as they were bidden. And then, stronger than all, there was the indifference to her of the man she loved!

Marie Bromar was a fine, high-spirited, animated girl; but it must not be thought that she was a highly educated lady, or that time had been given to her amidst all her occupations, in which she could allow her mind to dwell much on feelings of romance. Her life had ever been practical, busy, and full of action. As is ever the case with those who have to do chiefly with things material, she was thinking more frequently of the outer wants of those around her, than of the inner workings of her own heart and personal intelligence. Would the bread rise well? Would that bargain she had made for poultry suffice for the house? Was that lot of wine which she had persuaded her uncle to buy of a creditable quality? Were her efforts for increasing her uncle's profits compatible with satisfaction on the part of her uncle's guests? Such were the questions which from day to day occupied her attention and filled her with interest. And therefore her own identity was not strong to her, as it is strong to those whose business permits them to look frequently into themselves, or whose occupations are of a nature to produce such introspection. If her head ached, or had she lamed her hand by any accident, she would think more of the injury to the household arising from her incapacity than of her own pain. It is so, reader, with your gardener, your groom, or your cook, if you will think of it. Till you tell them by your pity that they are the sufferers, they will think that it is you who are most affected by their ailments. And the man who loses his daily wage because he is ill complains of his loss and not of his ailment. His own identity is half hidden from him by the practical wants of his life.

Had Marie been disappointed in her love without the appearance of any rival suitor, no one would have ever heard of her love. Had George Voss married, she would have gone on with her work without a sign of outward sorrow; or had he died, she would have wept for him with no peculiar tears. She did not expect much from the world around her, beyond this, that the guests should not complain about their suppers as long as the suppers provided were reasonably good. Had no great undertaking been presented to her, the performance of no heavy task demanded from her, she would have gone on with her work without showing even by the altered colour of her cheek that she was a sufferer. But this other man had come, - this Adrian Urmand; and a great undertaking was presented to her, and the performance of a heavy task was demanded from her. Then it was necessary that there should be identity of self and introspection. She had to ask herself whether the task was practicable, whether its performance was within the scope of her powers. She told herself at first that it was not to be done; that it was one which she would not even attempt. Then as she looked at it more frequently, as she came to understand how great was the urgency of her uncle; as she came to find, in performing that task of introspection, how unimportant a person she was herself, she began to think that the attempt might be made. 'I suppose it had better be so,' she had said. What was she that she should stand in the way of so many wishes? As she had worked for her bread in her uncle's house at Granpere, so would she work for her bread in her husband's house at Basle. No doubt there were other things to be joined to her work, - things the thought of which dismayed her. She had fought against them for a while; but, after all, what was she, that she should trouble the world by fighting? When she got to Basle she would endeavour to see that the bread should rise there, and the wine be sufficient, and the supper such as her husband might wish it to be.

Was it not the manifest duty of every girl to act after this fashion? Were not all marriages so arranged in the world around her? Among the Protestants of Alsace, as she knew, there was some greater latitude of choice than was ever allowed by the stricter discipline of Roman Catholic education. But then she was a Roman Catholic, as was her aunt; and she was too proud and too grateful to claim any peculiar exemption from the Protestantism of her uncle. She had resolved during those early hours of the morning that 'it had better be so.' She thought that she could go through with it all, if only they would not tease her, and ask her to wear her Sunday frock, and force her to sit down with them at table. Let them settle the day - with a word or two thrown in by herself to increase the distance - and she would be absolutely submissive, on condition that nothing should be required of her till the day should come. There would be a bad week or two then while she was being carried off to her new home; but she had looked forward and had told herself that she would fill her mind with the care of one man's house, as she had hitherto filled it with the care of the house of another man.

'So it is all right,' said her aunt, rushing up to her with warm congratulations, ready to flatter her, prone to admire her. It would be something to have a niece married to Adrian Urmand, the successful young merchant of Basle. Marie Bromar was already in her aunt's eyes something different from her former self.

'I hope so, aunt.'

'Hope so; but it is so, you have accepted him?'

'I hope it is right, I mean.'

'Of course it is right' said Madame Voss. 'How can it be wrong for a girl to accept the man whom all her friends wish her to marry? It must be right. And your uncle will be so happy.'

'Dear uncle!'

'Yes, indeed. He has been so good; and it has made me wretched to see that he has been disturbed. He has been as anxious that you should be settled well, as though you had been his own. And this will be to be settled well. I am told that M. Urmand's house is one of those which look down upon the river from near the church; the very best position in all the town. And it is full of everything, they say. His father spared nothing for furniture when he was married. And they say that his mother's linen was quite a sight to be seen. And then, Marie, everybody acknowledges that he is such a nice-looking young man!'

But it was not a part of Marie's programme to be waked up to enthusiasm - at any rate by her aunt. She said little or nothing, and would not even condescend to consider that interesting question, of the day of the wedding. 'There is quite time enough for all that, Aunt Josey,' she said, as she got up to go about her work. Aunt Josey was almost inclined to resent such usage, and would have done so, had not her respect for her niece been so great.

Michel did not return till near seven, and walking straight through his wife's room to Marie's seat of office, came upon his niece before he had seen any one else. There was an angry look about his brow, for he had been trying to teach himself that he was ill-used by his niece, in spite of that half-formed resolution to release her from persecution if she were still firm in her opposition to the marriage. 'Well,' he said, as soon as he saw her, - 'well, how is it to be?' She got off her stool, and coming close to him put up her face to be kissed. He understood it all in a moment, and the whole tone and colour of his countenance was altered. There was no man whose face would become more radiant with satisfaction than that of Michel Voss - when he was satisfied. Please him - and immediately there would be an effort on his part to please everybody around him. 'My darling, my own one,' he said, 'it is all right.' She kissed him again and pressed his arm, but said not a word. 'I am so glad,' he exclaimed; 'I am so glad!' And he knocked off his cap with his hand, not knowing what he was doing. 'We shall have but a poor house without you, Marie - a very poor house. But it is as it ought to be. I have felt for the last year or two, as you have sprung up to be such a woman among us, my dear, that there was only one place fit for such a one. It is proper that you should be mistress wherever you are. It has wounded me - I don't mind saying it now - it has wounded me to see you waiting on the sort of people that come here.'

'I have only been too happy, uncle, in doing it.'

'That's all very well; that's all very well, my dear. But I am older than you, and time goes quick with me. I tell you it made me unhappy. I thought I wasn't doing my duty by you. I was beginning to know that you ought to have a house and servants of your own. People say that it is a great match for you; but I tell them that it is a great match for him. Perhaps it is because you've been my own in a way, but I don't see any girl like you round the country.'

'You shouldn't say such things to flatter me, Uncle Michel.'

'I choose to say what I please, and think what I please, about my own girl,' he said, with his arm close wound round her. 'I say it's a great match for Adrian Urmand, and I am quite sure that he will not contradict me. He has had sense enough to know what sort of a young woman will make the best wife for him, and I respect him for it. I shall always respect Adrian Urmand because he has known better than to take up with one of your town-bred girls, who never learn anything except how to flaunt about with as much finery on their backs as they can get their people to give them. He might have had the pick of them at Basle, - or at Strasbourg either, for the matter of that; but he has thought my girl better than them all; and I love him for it - so I do. It was to be expected that a young fellow with means to please himself should choose to have a good-looking wife to sit at his table with him. Who'll blame him for that? And he has found the prettiest in all the country round. But he has wanted something more than good looks, - and he has got a great deal more. Yes; I say it, I, Michel Voss, though I am your uncle; - that he has got the pride of the whole country round. My darling, my own one, my child!'

All this was said with many interjections, and with sundry pauses in the speech, during which Michel caressed his niece, and pressed her to his breast, and signified his joy by all the outward modes of expression which a man so demonstrative knows how to use. This was a moment of great triumph to him, because he had begun to despair of success in this matter of the marriage, and had told himself on this very morning that the affair was almost hopeless. While he had been up in the wood, he had asked himself how he would treat Marie in consequence of her disobedience to him; and he had at last succeeded in producing within his own breast a state of mind that was not perhaps very reasonable, but which was consonant with his character. He would let her know that he was angry with her, - very angry with her; that she had half broken his heart by her obstinacy; but after that she should be to him his own Marie again. He would not throw her off, because she disobeyed him. He could not throw her off, because he loved her, and knew of no way by which he could get rid of his love. But he would be very angry, and she should know of his anger. He had come home wearing a black cloud on his brow, and intending to be black. But all that was changed in a moment, and his only thought now was how to give pleasure to this dear one. It is something to have a niece who brings such credit on the family!

Marie as she listened to his praise and his ecstasies, knowing by a sure instinct every turn of his thoughts, tried to take joy to herself in that she had given joy to him. Though he was her uncle, and had in fact been her master, he was actually the one real friend whom she had made for herself in her life. There had been a month or two of something more than friendship with George Voss; but she was too wise to look much at that now. Michel Voss was the one being in the world whom she knew best, of whom she thought most, whose thoughts and wishes she had most closely studied, whose interests were ever present to her mind. Perhaps it may be said of every human heart in a sound condition that it must be specially true to some other one human heart; but it may certainly be so said of every female heart. The object may be changed from time to time, - may be changed very suddenly, as when a girl's devotion is transferred with the consent of all her friends from her mother to her lover; or very slowly, as when a mother's is transferred from her husband to some favourite child; but, unless self-worship be predominant, there is always one friend to whom the woman's breast is true, - for whom it is the woman's joy to offer herself in sacrifice. Now with Marie Bromar that one being had been her uncle. She prospered, if he prospered. His comfort was her comfort. Even when his palate was pleased, there was some gratification akin to animal enjoyment on her part. It was ease to her, that he should be at his ease in his arm-chair. It was mirth to her, that he should laugh. When he was contented she was satisfied. When he was ruffled she was never smooth. Her sympathy with him was perfect; and now that he was radiant with triumph, though his triumph came from his victory over herself, she could not deny him the pleasure of triumphing with him.

'Dear uncle,' she said, still caressing him, 'I am so glad that you are pleased.'

'Of course it will be a poor house without you, Marie. As for me, it will be just as though I had lost my right leg and my right arm. But what! A man is not always to be thinking of himself. To see you treated by all the world as you ought to be treated, - as I should choose that my own daughter should be treated, - that is what I have desired. Sometimes when I've thought of it all when I've been alone, I have been mad with myself for letting it go on as it has done.'

'It has gone on very nicely, I think, Uncle Michel.' She knew how worse than useless it would be now to try and make him understand that it would be better for them both that she should remain with him. She knew, to the moving of a feather, what she could do with him and what she could not. Her immediate wish was to enable him to draw all possible pleasure from his triumph of the day, and therefore she would say no word to signify that his glory was founded on her sacrifice.

Then again came up the question of her position at supper, but there was no difficulty in the arrangement made between them. The one gala evening of grand dresses - the evening which had been intended to be a gala, but which had turned out to be almost funereal - was over. Even Michel Voss himself did not think it necessary that Marie should come in to supper with her silk dress two nights running; and he himself had found that that changing of his coat had impaired his comfort. He could eat his dinner and his supper in his best clothes on Sunday, and not feel the inconvenience; but on other occasions those unaccustomed garments were as heavy to him as a suit of armour. There was, therefore, nothing more said about clothes. Marie was to dispense her soup as usual, - expressing a confident assurance that if Peter were as yet to attempt this special branch of duty, the whole supper would collapse, - and then she was to take her place at the table, next to her uncle. Everybody in the house, everybody in Granpere, knew that the marriage had been arranged, and the old lady who had been so dreadfully snubbed by Marie, had forgiven the offence, acknowledging that Marie's position on that evening had been one of difficulty.

But these arrangements had reference only to two days. After two days, Adrian was to return to Basle, and to be seen no more at Granpere till he came to claim his bride. In regard to the choice of the day, Michel declared roundly that no constraint should be put upon Marie. She should have her full privileges, and no one should be allowed to interfere with her. On this point Marie had brought herself to be almost indifferent. A long engagement was a state of things which would have been quite incompatible with such a betrothal. Any delay that could have been effected would have been a delay, not of months, but of days, - or at most of a week or two. She had made up her mind that she would not be afraid of her wedding. She would teach herself to have no dread either of the man or of the thing. He was not a bad man, and marriage in itself was honourable. She formed ideas also of some future true friendship for her husband. She would endeavour to have a true solicitude for his interests, and would take care, at any rate, that nothing was squandered that came into her hands. Of what avail would it be to her that she should postpone for a few days the beginning of a friendship that was to last all her life? Such postponement could only be induced by a dread of the man, and she was firmly determined that she would not dread him. When they asked her, therefore, she smiled and said very little. What did her aunt think?

Her aunt thought that the marriage should be settled for the earliest possible day, - though she never quite expressed her thoughts. Madame Voss, though she did not generally obtain much credit for clear seeing, had a clearer insight to the state of her niece's mind than had her husband. She still believed that Marie's heart was not with Adrian Urmand. But, attributing perhaps no very great importance to a young girl's heart, and fancying that she knew that in this instance the young girl's heart could not have its own way, she was quite in favour of the Urmand marriage. And if they were to be married, the sooner the better. Of that she had no doubt. 'It's best to have it over always as soon as possible,' she said to her husband in private, nodding her head, and looking much wiser than usual.

'I won't have Marie hurried,' said Michel.

'We had better say some day next month, my dear,' said Madame Voss, again nodding her head. Michel, struck by the peculiarity of her voice, looked into her face, and saw the unaccustomed wisdom. He made no answer, but after a while nodded his head also, and went out of the room a man convinced. There were matters between women, he thought, which men can never quite understand. It would be very bad if there should be any slip here between the cup and the lip; and, no doubt, his wife was right.

It was Madame Voss at last who settled the day, - the 15th of October, just four weeks from the present time. This she did in concert with Adrian Urmand, who, however, was very docile in her hands. Urmand, after he had been accepted, soon managed to bring himself back to that state of mind in which he had before regarded the possession of Marie Bromar as very desirable. For some four-and-twenty hours, during which he had thought himself to be ill-used, and had meditated a retreat from Granpere, he had contrived to teach himself that he might possibly live without her; but as soon as he was accepted, and when the congratulations of the men and women of Granpere were showered down upon him in quick succession, - so that the fact that the thing was to be became assured to him, - he soon came to fancy again that he was a man as successful in love as he was in the world's good, and that this acquisition of Marie's hand was a treasure in which he could take delight. He undoubtedly would be ready by the day named, and would go home and prepare everything for Marie's arrival.

They were very little together as lovers during those two days, but it was necessary that there should be an especial parting. 'She is up-stairs in the little sitting-room,' Aunt Josey said; and up-stairs to the little sitting-room Adrian Urmand went.

'I am come to say good-bye,' said Urmand.

'Good-bye, Adrian,' said Marie, putting both her hands in his, and offering her cheek to be kissed.

'I shall come back with such joy for the 15th,' said he.

She smiled, and kissed his cheek, and still held his hand. 'Adrian,' she said.

'My love?'

'As I believe in the dear Jesus, I will do my best to be a good wife to you.' Then he took her in his arms, and kissed her close, and went out of the room with tears streaming down his cheeks. He knew now that he was in truth a happy man, and that God had been good to him in this matter of his future wife.

Chapter 10

'So your cousin Marie is to be married to Adrian Urmand, the young linen-merchant at Basle,' said Madame Faragon one morning to George Voss. In this manner were the first assured tidings of the coming marriage conveyed to the rival lover. This occurred a day or two after the betrothal, when Adrian was back at Basle. No one at Granpere had thought of writing an express letter to George on the subject. George's father might have done so, had the writing of letters been a customary thing with him; but his correspondence was not numerous, and such letters as he did write were short, and always confined to matters concerning his trade. Madame Voss had, however, sent a special message to Madame Faragon, as soon as Adrian had gone, thinking that it would be well that in this way George should learn the truth.

It had been fully arranged by this time that George Voss was to be the landlord of the hotel at Colmar on and from the first day of the following year. Madame Faragon was to be allowed to sit in the little room downstairs, to scold the servants, and to make the strangers from a distance believe that her authority was unimpaired. She was also to receive a moderate annual pension in money in addition to her board and lodging. For these considerations, and on condition that George Voss should expend a certain sum of money in renewing the faded glories of the house, he was to be the landlord in full enjoyment of all real power on the first of January following. Madame Faragon, when she had expressed her agreement to the arrangement, which was indeed almost in all respects one of her own creation, wept and wheezed and groaned bitterly. She declared that she would soon be dead, and so trouble him no more. Nevertheless, she especially stipulated that she should have a new arm-chair for her own use, and that the feather bed in her own chamber should be renewed.

'So your cousin Marie is to be married to Adrian Urmand, the young linen-merchant at Basle,' said Madame Faragon.

'Who says so?' demanded George. He asked his question in a quiet voice; but, though the news had reached him thus suddenly, he had sufficient control over himself to prevent any plain expression of his feelings. The thing which had been told him had gone into his heart like a knife; but he did not intend that Madame Faragon should know that he had been wounded.

'It is quite true. There is no doubt about it. Stodel's man with the roulage brought me word direct from your step-mother.' George immediately began to inquire within himself why Stodel's man with the roulage had not brought some word direct to him, and answered the question to himself not altogether incorrectly. 'O, yes,' continued Madame Faragon, 'it is quite true - on the 15th of October. I suppose you will be going over to the wedding.' This she said in her usual whining tone of small complaint, signifying thereby how great would be the grievance to herself to be left alone at that special time.

'I shall not go to the wedding,' said George. 'They can be married, if they are to be married, without me.'

'They are to be married; you may be quite sure of that.' Madame Faragon's grievance now consisted in the amount of doubt which was being thrown on the tidings which had been sent direct to her. 'Of course you will choose to have a doubt, because it is I who tell you.'

'I do not doubt it at all. I think it is very likely. I was well aware before that my father wished it.'

'Of course he would wish it, George. How should he not wish it? Marie Bromar never had a franc of her own in her life, and it is not to be expected that he, with a family of young children at his heels, is to give her a *dot*.'

'He will give her something. He will treat her as though she were a daughter.'

'Then I think he ought not. But your father was always a romantic, headstrong man. At any rate, there she is, - bar-maid, as we may say, in the hotel, - much the same as our Floschen here; and, of course, such a marriage as this is a great thing; a very great thing, indeed. How should they not wish it?'

'O, if she likes him - !'

83

'Like him? Of course, she will like him. Why should she not like him? Young, and good-looking, with a fine business, doesn't owe a sou, I'll be bound, and with a houseful of furniture. Of course, she'll like him. I don't suppose there is so much difficulty about that.'

'I daresay not,' said George. 'I believe that women's likings go after that fashion, for the most part.'

Madame Faragon, not understanding this general sarcasm against her sex, continued the expression of her opinion about the coming marriage. 'I don't suppose anybody will think of blaming Marie Bromar for accepting the match when it was proposed to her. Of course, she would do as she was bidden, and could hardly be expected to say that the man was above her.'

'He is not above her,' said George in a hoarse voice.

'Marie Bromar is nothing to you, George; nothing in blood; nothing beyond a most distant cousin. They do say that she has grown up good-looking.'

'Yes; - she is a handsome girl.'

'When I remember her as a child she was broad and dumpy, and they always come back at last to what they were as children. But of course M. Urmand only looks to what she is now. She makes her hay while the sun shines; but I hope the people won't say that your father has caught him at the Lion d'Or, and taken him in.'

'My father is not the man to care very much what anybody says about such things.'

'Perhaps not so much as he ought, George,' said Madame Faragon, shaking her head.

After that George Voss went about the house for some hours, doing his work, giving his orders, and going through the usual routine of his day's business. As he did so, no one guessed that his mind was disturbed. Madame Faragon had not the slightest suspicion that the matter of Marie's marriage was a cause of sorrow to him. She had felt the not unnatural envy of a woman's mind in such an affair, and could not help expressing it, although Marie Bromar was in some sort connected with herself. But she was sure that such an arrangement would be regarded as a family triumph by George, - unless, indeed, he should be inclined to quarrel with his father for over-generosity in that matter of the *dot*. 'It is lucky that you got your little bit of money before this affair was settled,' said she.

'It would not have made the difference of a copper sou,' said George Voss, as he walked angrily out of the old woman's room. This was in the evening, after supper, and the greater part of the day had passed since he had first heard the news. Up to the present moment he had endeavoured to shake the matter off from him, declaring to himself that grief - or at least any outward show of grief - would be unmanly and unworthy of him. With a strong resolve he had fixed his mind upon the affairs of his house, and had allowed himself to meditate as little as might be possible. But the misery, the agony, had been then present with him during all those hours, - and had been made the sharper by his endeavours to keep it down and banish it from his thoughts. Now, as he went out from Madame Faragon's room, having finished all that it was his duty to do, he strolled into the town, and at once began to give way to his thoughts. Of course he must think about it. He acknowledged that it was useless for him to attempt to get rid of the matter and let it be as though there were no such persons in the world as Marie Bromar and Adrian Urmand. He must think about it; but he might so give play to his feelings that no one should see him in the moments of his wretchedness. He went out, therefore, among the dark walks in the town garden, and there, as he paced one alley after another in the gloom, he revelled in the agony which a passionate man feels when the woman whom he loves is to be given into the arms of another.

As he thought of his own life during the past year or fifteen months, he could not but tell himself that his present suffering was due in some degree to his own fault. If he really loved this girl, and if it had been his intention to try and win her for himself, why had he taken his father at his word and gone away from Granpere? And why, having left Granpere, had he taken no trouble to let her know that he still loved her? As he asked himself these questions, he was hardly able himself to understand the pride which had driven him away from his old home, and which had kept him silent so long. She had promised him that she would be true to him. Then had come those few words from his father's mouth, words which he thought his father should never have spoken to him, and he had gone away, telling himself that he would come back and fetch her as soon as he could offer her a home independently of his father. If, after the promises she had made to him, she would not wait for him without farther words and farther vows, she would not be worth the having. In going, he had not precisely told himself that there should be no intercourse between them for twelve months; but the silence which he had maintained, and his continued absence, had been the consequence of the mood of his mind and the tenor of his purpose. The longer he had been away from Granpere without tidings from any one there, the less possible had it been that he should send tidings from himself to his old home. He had not expected messages. He had not expected any letter. But when nothing came, he told himself over and over again that he too would be silent, and would bide his time. Then Edmond Greisse had come to Colmar, and brought the first rumour of Adrian Urmand's proposal of marriage.

The reader will perhaps remember that George, when he heard this first rumour, had at once made up his mind to go over to Granpere, and that he went. He went to Granpere partly believing, and partly disbelieving Edmond's story. If it were untrue, perhaps she might say a word to him that would comfort him and give him new hope. If it were true, she would have to tell him so; and then he would say a word to her that should tear her heart, if her heart was to be reached. But he would never let her know that she had torn his own to rags! That was the pride of his manliness; and yet he was so boyish as not to know that it should have been for him to make those overtures for a renewal of love, which he hoped that Marie would make to him. He had gone over to Granpere, and the reader will perhaps again remember what had passed then between him and Marie. Just as he was leaving her he had asked her whether she was to be married to this man. He had made no objection to such a marriage. He had spoken no word of the constancy of his own affection. In his heart there had been anger against her because she had spoken no such word to him, - as of course there was also in her heart against him, very bitter and very hot. If he wished her to be true to him, why did he not say so? If he had given her up, why did he come there at all? Why did he ask any questions about her marriage, if on his own behalf he had no statement to make, - no assurance to give? What was her marriage, or her refusal to be married, to him? Was she to tell him that, as he had deserted her, and as she could not busy herself to overcome her love, therefore she was minded to wear the willow for ever? 'If my uncle and aunt choose to dispose of me, I cannot help it,' she had said. Then he had left her, and she had been sure that for him that early game of love was a game altogether played out. Now, as he walked along the dark paths of the town garden, something of the truth came upon him. He made no excuse for Marie Bromar. She had given him a vow, and should have been true to her vow, so he said to himself a dozen times. He had never been false. He had shown no sign of falseness. True of heart, he had remained away from her only till he might come and claim her, and bring her to a house that he could call his own. This also he told himself a dozen times. But, nevertheless, there was a very agony of remorse, a weight of repentance, in that he had not striven to make sure of his prize when he had been at Granpere before the marriage was settled. Had she loved him as she ought to have loved him, had she loved him as he loved her, there should have been no question possible to her of marriage with another man. But still he repented, in that he had lost that which he desired, and might perhaps have then obtained it for himself.

But the strong feeling of his breast, the strongest next to his love, was a desire to be revenged. He cared little now for his father, little for that personal dignity which he had intended to return by his silence, little for pecuniary advantages and prudential motives, in comparison with his strong desire to punish Marie for her perfidy. He would go over to Granpere, and fall among them like a thunderbolt. Like a thunderbolt, at any rate, he would fall upon the head of Marie Bromar. The very words of her love-promises were still firm in his memory, and he would see if she also could be made to remember them.

'I shall go over to Granpere the day after to-morrow,' he said to Madame Faragon, as he caught her just before she retired for the night.

'To Granpere the day after to-morrow? And why?'

'Well, I don't know that I can say exactly why. I shall not be at the marriage, but I should like to see them first. I shall go the day after to-morrow.'

And he went to Granpere on the day he fixed.

Chapter 11

'Probably one night only, but I won't make any promise,' George had said to Madame Faragon when she asked him how long he intended to stay at Granpere. As he took one of the horses belonging to the inn and drove himself, it seemed to be certain that he would not stay long. He started all alone, early in the morning, and reached Granpere about twelve o'clock. His mind was full of painful thoughts as he went, and as the little animal ran quickly down the mountain road into the valley in which Granpere lies, he almost wished that his feet were not so fleet. What was he to say when he got to Granpere, and to whom was he to say it?

When he reached the angular court along two sides of which the house was built he did not at once enter the front door. None of the family were then about the place, and he could, therefore, go into the stable and ask a question or two of the man who came to meet him. His father, the man told him, had gone up early to the wood-cutting, and would not probably return till the afternoon. Madame Voss was no doubt inside, as was also Marie Bromar. Then the man commenced an elaborate account of the betrothals. There never had been at Granpere any marriage that had been half so important as would be this marriage; no lover coming thither had ever been blessed with so beautiful and discreet a maiden, and no maiden of Granpere had ever before had at her feet a lover at the same time so good-looking, so wealthy, so sagacious, and so good-tempered. The man declared that Adrian was the luckiest fellow in the world in finding such a wife, but his enthusiasm rose to the highest pitch when he spoke of Marie's luck in finding such a husband. There was no end to the good with which she would be endowed - 'linen,' said the man, holding up his hands in admiration, 'that will last out all her grandchildren at least!' George listened to it all, and smiled, and said a word or two -

was it worth his while to come all the way to Granpere to throw his thunderbolt at a girl who had been captivated by promises of a chest full of house linen!

George told the man that he would go up to the wood-cutting after his father; but before he was out of the court he changed his mind and slowly entered the house. Why should he go to his father? What had he to say to his father about the marriage that could not be better said down at the house? After all, he had but little ground of complaint against his father. It was Marie who had been untrue to him, and it was on Marie's head that his wrath must fall. No doubt his father would be angry with him when he should have thrown his thunderbolt. It could not, as he thought, be hurled effectually without his father's knowledge; but he need not tell his father the errand on which he had come. So he changed his mind, and went into the inn.

He entered the house almost dreading to see her whom he was seeking. In what way should he first express his wrath? How should he show her the wreck which by her inconstancy she had made of his happiness? His first words must, if possible, be spoken to her alone; and yet alone he could hardly hope to find her. And he feared her. Though he was so resolved to speak his mind, yet he feared her. Though he intended to fill her with remorse, yet he dreaded the effect of her words upon himself. He knew how strong she could be, and how steadfast. Though his passion told him every hour, was telling him all day long, that she was as false as hell, yet there was something in him of judgment, something rather of instinct, which told him also that she was not bad, that she was a firm-hearted, high-spirited, great-minded girl, who would have reasons to give for the thing that she was doing.

He went through into the kitchen before he met any one, and there he found Madame Voss with the cook and Peter. Immediate explanations had, of course, to be made as to his unexpected arrival; - questions asked, and suggestions offered - 'Came he in peace, or came he in war?' Had he come because he had heard of the betrothals? He admitted that it was so. 'And you are glad of it?' asked Madame Voss. 'You will congratulate her with all your heart?'

'I will congratulate her certainly,' said George. Then the cook and Peter began with a copious flow of domestic eloquence to declare how great a marriage this was for the Lion d'Or - how pleasing to the master, how creditable to the village, how satisfactory to the friends, how joyous to the bridegroom, how triumphant to the bride! 'No doubt she will have plenty to eat and drink, and fine clothes to wear, and an excellent house over her head,' said George in his bitterness.

'And she will be married to one of the most respectable young men in all Switzerland,' said Madame Voss in a tone of much anger. It was already quite clear to Madame Voss, to the cook, and to Peter, that George had not come over from Colmar simply to express his joyous satisfaction at his cousin's good fortune.

He soon walked through into the little sitting-room, and his step-mother followed him. 'George,' she said, 'you will displease your father very much if you say anything unkind about Marie.'

'I know very well,' said he, 'that my father cares more for Marie than he does for me.'

'That is not so, George.'

'I do not blame him for it. She lives in the house with him, while I live elsewhere. It was natural that she should be more to him than I am, after he had sent me away. But he has no right to suppose that I can have the same feeling that he has about this marriage. I cannot think it the finest thing in the world for all of us that Marie Bromar should succeed in getting a rich young man for her husband, who, as far as I can see, never had two ideas in his head.'

'He is a most industrious young man, who thoroughly understands his business. I have heard people say that there is no one comes to Granpere who can buy better than he can.'

'Very likely not.'

'And at any rate, it is no disgrace to be well off.'

'It is a disgrace to think more about that than anything else. But never mind. It is no use talking about it, words won't mend it.'

'Why then have you come here now?'

'Because I want to see my father.' Then he remembered how false was this excuse; and remembered also how soon its falseness would appear. 'Besides, though I do not like this match, I wish to see Marie once again before her marriage. I shall never see her after it. That is the reason why I have come. I suppose you can give me a bed.'

'O, yes, there are beds enough.' After that there was some pause, and Madame Voss hardly knew how to treat her stepson. At last she asked him whether he would have dinner, and an order was given to Peter to prepare something for the young master in the small room. And George asked after the children, and in this way the dreaded subject was for some minutes laid on one side.

In the mean time, information of George's arrival had been taken upstairs to Marie. She had often wondered what sign he would make when he should hear of her engagement. Would he send her a word of affection, or such customary present as would be usual between two persons so nearly connected? Would he come to her marriage? And what would be his own feelings? She too remembered well, with absolute accuracy, those warm, delicious, heavenly words of love which had passed between them. She could feel now the pressure of his hand and the warmth of his kiss, when she swore to him that she would be his for ever and ever. After that he had left her, and for a year had sent no token. Then he had come again, and had simply asked her whether she were engaged to another man; had asked with a cruel indication that he at least intended that the old childish words should be forgotten. Now he was in the house again, and she would have to hear his congratulations!

She thought for some quarter of an hour what she had better do, and then she determined to go down to him at once. The sooner the first meeting was over the better. Were she to remain away from him till they should be brought together at the supper-table, there would almost be a necessity for her to explain her conduct. She would go down to him and treat him exactly as she might have done, had there never been any special love between them. She would do so as perfectly as her strength might enable her; and if she failed in aught, it would be better to fail before her aunt than in the presence of her uncle. When she had resolved, she waited yet another minute or two, and then she went down-stairs.

As she entered her aunt's room George Voss was sitting before the stove, while Madame Voss was in her accustomed chair, and Peter was preparing the table for his young master's dinner. George arose from his seat at once, and then came a look of pain across his face. Marie saw it at once, and almost loved him the more because he suffered. 'I am so glad to see you, George,' she said. 'I am so glad that you have come.'

She had offered him her hand, and of course he had taken it. 'Yes,' he said, 'I thought it best just to run over. We shall be very busy at the hotel before long.'

'Does that mean to say that you are not to be here for my marriage?' This she said with her sweetest smile, making all the effort in her power to give a gracious tone to her voice. It was better, she knew, to plunge at the subject at once.

'No,' said he. 'I shall not be here then.'

'Ah, - your father will miss you so much! But if it cannot be, it is very good of you to come now. There would have been something sad in going away from the old house without seeing you once more. And though Colmar and Basle are very near, it will not be the same as in the dear old home; - will it, George?' There was a touch about her voice as she called him by his name, that nearly killed him. At that moment his hatred was strongest against Adrian. Why had such an upstart as that, a puny, miserable creature, come between him and the only thing that he had ever seen in the guise of a woman that could touch his heart? He turned round with his back to the table and his face to the stove, and said nothing. But he was able, when he no longer saw her, when her voice was not sounding in his ear, to swear that the thunderbolt should be hurled all the same. His journey to Granpere should not be made for nothing. 'I must go now,' she said presently. 'I shall see you at supper, shall I not, George, when Uncle will be with us? Uncle Michel will be so delighted to find you. And you will tell us of the new doings at the hotel. Good-bye for the present, George.' Then she was gone before he had spoken another word.

He eat his dinner, and smoked a cigar about the yard, and then said that he would go out and meet his father. He did go out, but did not take the road by which he knew that his father was to be found. He strolled off to the ravine, and came back only when it was dark. The meeting between him and his father was kindly; but there was no special word spoken, and thus they all sat down to supper.

Chapter 12

It became necessary as George Voss sat at supper with his father and Madame Voss that he should fix the time of his return to Colmar, and he did so for the early morning of the next day but one. He had told Madame Faragon that he expected to stay at Granpere but one night. He felt, however, after his arrival that it might be difficult for him to get away on the following day, and therefore he told them that he would sleep two nights at the Lion d'Or, and then start early, so as to reach the Colmar inn by mid-day.

'I suppose you find the old lady rather fidgety, George?' said Michel Voss in high good humour.

George found it easier to talk about Madame Faragon and the hotel at Colmar than he did of things at Granpere, and therefore became communicative as to his own affairs. Michel too preferred the subject of the new doings at the house on the other side of the Vosges. His wife had given him a slight hint, doing her best, like a good wife and discreet manager, to prevent ill-humour and hard words.

'He feels a little sore, you know. I was always sure there was something. But it was wise of him to come and see her, and it will go off in this way.'

Michel swore that George had no right to be sore, and that if his son did not take pride in such a family arrangement as this, he should no longer be son of his. But he allowed himself to be counselled by his wife, and soon talked himself into a pleasant mood, discussing Madame Faragon, and the horses belonging to the Hôtel de la Poste, and Colmar affairs in general. There was a certain important ground for satisfaction between them. Everybody agreed that George Voss had shown himself to be a steady man of business in the affairs of the inn at Colmar.

Marie Bromar in the mean while went on with her usual occupation round the room, but now and again came and stood at

94

her uncle's elbow, joining in the conversation, and asking a question or two about Madame Faragon. There was, perhaps, something of the guile of the serpent joined to her dove-like softness. She asked questions and listened to answers - not that in her present state of mind she could bring herself to take a deep interest in the affairs of Madame Faragon's hotel, but because it suited her that there should be some subject of easy conversation between her and George. It was absolutely necessary now that George should be nothing more to her than a cousin and an acquaintance; but it was well that he should be that and not an enemy. It would be well too that he should know, that he should think that he knew, that she was disturbed by no remembrance of those words which had once passed between them. At last she trusted herself to a remark which perhaps she would not have made had the serpent's guile been more perfect of its kind.

'Surely you must get a wife, George, as soon as the house is your own.'

'Of course he will get a wife,' said the father.

'I hope he will get a good one,' said Madame Voss after a short pause - which, however, had been long enough to make her feel it necessary to say something.

George said never a word, but lifted his glass and finished his wine. Marie at once perceived that the subject was one on which she must not venture to touch again. Indeed, she saw farther than that, and became aware that it would be inexpedient for her to fall into any special or minute conversation with her cousin during his short stay at Granpere.

'You'll go up to the woods with me tomorrow - eh, George?' said the father. The son of course assented. It was hardly possible that he should not assent. The whole day, moreover, would not be wanted for that purpose of throwing his thunderbolt; and if he could get it thrown, it would be well that he should be as far away from Marie as possible for the remainder of his visit. 'We'll start early, Marie, and have a bit of breakfast before we go. Will six be too early for you, George, with your town ways?' George said that six would not be too early, and as he made the engagement for the morning he resolved that he would if possible throw his thunderbolt that night. 'Marie will get us a cup of coffee and a sausage. Marie is always up by that time.'

Marie smiled, and promised that they should not be compelled to start upon their walk with empty stomachs from any fault of hers. If a hot breakfast at six o'clock in the morning could put her cousin into a good humour, it certainly should not be wanting.

In two hours after supper George was with his father. Michel was so full of happiness and so confidential that the son found it very difficult to keep silence about his own sorrow. Had it not been that with a half obedience to his wife's hints Michel said little about Adrian, there must have been an explosion. He endeavoured to confine himself to George's prospects, as to which he expressed himself thoroughly pleased. 'You see,' said he, 'I am so strong of my years, that if you wished for my shoes, there is no knowing how long you might be kept waiting.'

'It couldn't have been too long,' said George.

'Ah well, I don't believe you would have been impatient to put the old fellow under the sod. But I should have been impatient, I should have been unhappy. You might have had the woods, to be sure; but it's hardly enough of a business alone. Besides, a young man is always more his own master away from his father. I can understand that. The only thing is, George, - take a drive over, and see us sometimes.' This was all very well, but it was not quite so well when he began to speak of Marie. 'It's a terrible loss her going, you know, George; I shall feel it sadly.'

'I can understand that,' said George.

'But of course I had my duty to do to the girl. I had to see that she should be well settled, and she will be well settled. There's a comfort in that; - isn't there, George?'

But George could not bring himself to reply to this with good-humoured zeal, and there came for a moment a cloud between the father and son. But Michel was wise and swallowed his wrath, and in a minute or two returned to Colmar and Madame Faragon.

At about half-past nine George escaped from his father and returned to the house. They had been sitting in the balcony which runs round the billiard-room on the side of the court opposite to the front door. He returned to the house, and caught Marie in one of the passages up-stairs, as she was completing her work for the day. He caught her close to the door of his own room and asked her to come in, that he might speak a word to her. English readers will perhaps remember that among the Vosges mountains there is less of a sense of privacy attached to bedrooms than is the case with us here in England. Marie knew immediately then that her cousin had not come to Granpere for nothing, - had not come with the innocent intention of simply pleasing his father, - had not come to say an ordinary word of farewell to her before her marriage. There was to be something of a scene, though she could not tell of what nature the scene might be. She knew, however, that her own conduct had been right; and therefore, though she would have avoided the scene, had it been possible, she would not fear it. She went into his room; and when he closed the door, she smiled, and did not as yet tremble.

'Marie,' he said, 'I have come here on purpose to say a word or two to you.' There was no smile on her face as he spoke now. The intention to be savage was written there, as plainly as any purpose was ever written on man's countenance. Marie read the writing without missing a letter. She was to be rebuked, and sternly rebuked; - rebuked by the man who had taken her heart, and then left her; - rebuked by the man who had crushed her hopes and made it absolutely necessary for her to give up all the sweet poetry of her life, to forget her dreams, to abandon every wished-for prettiness of existence, and confine herself to duties and to things material! He who had so sinned against her was about to rid himself of the burden of his sin by endeavouring to cast it upon her. So much she understood, but yet she did not understand all that was to come. She would hear the rebuke as quietly as she might. In the interest of others she would do so. But she would not fear him, - and she would say a quiet word in defence of her own sex if there should be need. Such was the purport of her mind as she stood opposite to him in his room.

'I hope they will be kind words,' she said. 'As we are to part so soon, there should be none unkind spoken.'

'I do not know much about kindness,' he replied. Then he paused and tried to think how best the thunderbolt might be hurled. 'There is hardly room for kindness where there was once so much more than kindness; where there was so much more, - or the pretence of it.' Then he waited again, as though he expected that she should speak. But she would not speak at all. If he had aught to say, let him say it. 'Perhaps, Marie, you have in truth forgotten all the promises you once made me?' Though this was a direct question she would not answer it. Her words to him should be as few as possible, and the time for such words had not come as yet. 'It suits you no doubt to forget them now, but I cannot forget them. You have been false to me, and have broken my heart. You have been false to me, when my only joy on earth was in believing in your truth. Your vow was for ever and ever, and within one short year you are betrothed to another man! And why? - because they tell you that he is rich and has got a house full of furniture! You may prove to be a blessing to his house. Who can say? On mine, you and your memory will be a curse, - lasting all my lifetime!' And so the thunderbolt had been hurled.

And it fell as a thunderbolt. What she had expected had not been at all like to this. She had known that he would rebuke her; but, feeling strong in her own innocence and her own purity, knowing or thinking that she knew that the fault had all been his, not believing - having got rid of all belief - that he still loved her, she had fancied that his rebuke would be unjust, cruel, but bearable. Nay; she had thought that she could almost triumph over him with a short word of reply. She had expected from him reproach, but not love. There was reproach indeed, but it came with an expression of passion of which she had not known him to be capable. He stood before her telling her that she had broken his heart, and, as he told her so, his words were half choked by sobs. He reminded her of her promises, declaring that his own to her had ever remained in full force. And he told her that she, she to whom he had looked for all his joy, had become a curse to him and a blight upon his life. There were thoughts and feelings too beyond all these that crowded themselves upon her heart and upon her mind at the moment. It had been possible for her to accept the hand of Adrian Urmand because she had become assured that George Voss no longer regarded her as his promised bride. She would have stood firm against her uncle and her aunt, she would have stood against all the world, had it not seemed to her that the evidence of her cousin's indifference was complete. Had not that evidence been complete at all points, it would have been impossible to her to think of becoming the wife of another man. Now the evidence on that matter which had seemed to her to be so sufficient was all blown to the winds.

It is true that had all her feelings been guided by reason only, she might have been as strong as ever. In truth she had not sinned against him. In truth she had not sinned at all. She had not done that which she herself had desired. She had not been anxious for wealth, or ease, or position; but had, after painful thought, endeavoured to shape her conduct by the wishes of others, and by her ideas of duty, as duty had been taught to her. O, how willingly would she have remained as servant to her uncle, and have allowed M. Urmand to carry the rich gift of his linen-chest to the feet of some other damsel, had she believed herself to be free to choose! Had there been no passion in her heart, she would now have known herself to be strong in duty, and would have been able to have answered and to have borne the rebuke of her old lover. But passion was there, hot within her, aiding every word as he spoke it, giving strength to his complaints, telling her of all that she had lost, telling her of all she had taken from him. She forgot to remember now that he had been silent for a year. She forgot now to think of the tone in which he had asked about her marriage when no such marriage was in her mind. But she remembered well the promise she had made, and the words of it. 'Your vow was for ever and ever.' When she heard those words repeated from his lips, her heart too was broken. All idea of holding herself before him as one injured but ready to forgive was gone from her. If by falling at his feet and owning herself to be vile and mansworn she might get his pardon, she was ready now to lie there on the ground before him.

'O George!' she said; 'O George!'

'What is the use of that now?' he replied, turning away from her. He had thrown his thunderbolt, and he had nothing more to say. He had seen that he had not thrown it quite in vain, and he would have been contented to be away and back at Colmar. What more was there to be said?

She came to him very gently, very humbly, and just touched his arm with her hand. 'Do you mean, George, that you have continued to care for me - always?'

'Care for you? I know not what you call caring. Did I not swear to you that I would love you for ever and ever, and that you should be my own? Did I not leave this house and go away, - till I could earn for you one that should be fit for you, - because I loved you? Why should I have broken my word? I do not believe that you thought that it was broken.'

'By my God, that knows me, I did!' As she said this she burst into tears and fell on her knees at his feet.

'Marie,' he said, 'Marie; - there is no use in this. Stand up.'

'Not till you tell me that you will forgive me. By the name of the good Jesus, who knows all our hearts, I thought that you had forgotten me. O George, if you could know all! If you could know how I have loved you; how I have sorrowed from day to day because I was forgotten! How I have struggled to bear it, telling myself that you were away, with all the world to interest you, and not like me, a poor girl in a village, with nothing to think of but my lover! How I have striven to do my duty by my uncle, and have obeyed him, because, - because, - because, there was nothing left. If you could know it all! If you could know it all!' Then she clasped her arms round his legs, and hid her face upon his feet.

'And whom do you love now?' he asked. She continued to sob, but did not answer him a word. Then he stooped down and raised her to her feet, and she stood beside him, very near to him with her face averted. 'And whom do you love now?' he asked again. 'Is it me, or is it Adrian Urmand?' But she could not answer him, though she had said enough in her passionate sorrow to make any answer to such a question unnecessary, as far as knowledge on the subject might be required. It might suit his views that she should confess the truth in so many words, but for other purpose her answer had been full enough. 'This is very sad,' he said, 'sad indeed; but I thought that you would have been firmer.'

'Do not chide me again, George.'

'No; - it is to no purpose.'

'You said that I was - a curse to you?'

'O Marie, I had hoped, - I had so hoped, that you would have been my blessing!'

'Say that I am not a curse to you, George!'

But he would make no answer to this appeal, no immediate answer; but stood silent and stern, while she stood still touching his arm, waiting in patience for some word at any rate of forgiveness. He was using all the powers of his mind to see if there might even yet be any way to escape this great shipwreck. She had not answered his question. She had not told him in so many words that her heart was still his, though she had promised her hand to the Basle merchant. But he could not doubt that it was so. As he stood there silent, with that dark look upon his brow which he had inherited from his father, and that angry fire in his eye, his heart was in truth once more becoming soft and tender towards her. He was beginning to understand how it had been with her. He had told her, just now, that he did not believe her, when she assured him that she had thought that she was forgotten. Now he did believe her. And there arose in his breast a feeling that it was due to her that he should explain this change in his mind. 'I suppose you did think it,' he said suddenly.

'Think what, George?'

'That I was a vain, empty, false-tongued fellow, whose word was worth no reliance.'

'I thought no evil of you, George, - except that you were changed to me. When you came, you said nothing to me. Do you not remember?'

'I came because I was told that you were to be married to this man. I asked you the question, and you would not deny it. Then I said to myself that I would wait and see.' When he had spoken she had nothing farther to say to him. The charges which he made against her were all true. They seemed at least to be true to her then in her present mood, - in that mood in which all that she now desired was his forgiveness. The wish to defend herself, and to stand before him as one justified, had gone from her. She felt that having still possessed his love, having still been the owner of the one thing that she valued, she had ruined herself by her own doubts; and she could not forgive herself the fatal blunder. 'It is of no use to think of it any more,' he said at last. 'You have to become this man's wife now, and I suppose you must go through with it.'

'I suppose I must,' she said; 'unless - '

'Unless what?'

'Nothing, George. Of course I will marry him. He has my word. And I have promised my uncle also. But, George, you will say that you forgive me?'

'Yes; - I will forgive you.' But still there was the same black cloud upon his face, - the same look of pain, - the same glance of anger in his eye.

'O George, I am so unhappy! There can be no comfort for me now, unless you will say that you will be contented.'

'I cannot say that, Marie.'

'You will have your house, and your business, and so many things to interest you. And in time, - after a little time - '

'No, Marie, after no time at all. You told me at supper to-night that I had better get a wife for myself. But I will get no wife. I could not bring myself to marry another girl, I could not take a woman home as my wife if I did not love her. If she were not the person of all persons most dear to me, I should loathe her.'

He was speaking daggers to her, and he must have known how sharp were his words. He was speaking daggers to her, and she must have felt that he knew how he was wounding her. But yet she did not resent his usage, even by a motion of her lip. Could she have brought herself to do so, her agony would have been less sharp. 'I suppose,' she said at last, 'that a woman is weaker than a man. But you say that you will forgive me?'

'I have forgiven you.'

Then very gently she put out her hand to him, and he took it and held it for a minute. She looked up at him as though for a moment she had thought that there might be something else, - that there might be some other token of true forgiveness, and then she withdrew her hand. 'I had better go now,' she said. 'Good-night; George.'

'Good-night, Marie.' And then she was gone.

As soon as he was alone he sat himself down on the bedside, and began to think of it. Everything was changed to him since he had called her into the room, determining that he would

102

crush her with his thunderbolt. Let things go as they may with a man in an affair of love, let him be as far as possible from the attainment of his wishes, there will always be consolation to him if he knows that he is loved. To be preferred to all others, even though that preference may lead to no fruition, is in itself a thing enjoyable. He had believed that Marie had forgotten him, - that she had been captivated either by the effeminate prettiness of his rival, or by his wealth and standing in the world. He believed all this no more. He knew now how it was with her and with him, and, let his countenance say what it might to the contrary, he could bring himself to forgive her in his heart. She had not forgotten him! She had not ceased to love him! There was merit in that which went far with him in excuse of her perfidy.

But what should he do now? She was not as yet married to Adrian Urmand. Might there not still be hope; hope for her sake as well as for his own? He perfectly understood that in his country - nay, for aught he knew to the contrary, in all countries - a formal betrothal was half a marriage. It was half the ceremony in the eyes of all those concerned; but yet, in regard to that indissoluble bond which would indeed have divided Marie from him beyond the reach of any hope to the contrary, such betrothal was of no effect whatever. This man whom she did not love was not yet Marie's husband; - need never become so if Marie could only be sufficiently firm in resisting the influence of all her friends. No priest could marry her without her own consent. He - George - he himself would have to face the enmity of all those with whom he was connected. He was sure that his father, having been a party to the betrothal, would never consent to a breach of his promise to Urmand. Madame Voss, Madame Faragon, the priest, and their Protestant pastor would all be against them. They would be as it were outcasts from their own family. But George Voss, sitting there on his bedside, thought that he could go through it all, if only he could induce Marie Bromar to bear the brunt of the world's displeasure with him. As he got into bed he determined that he would begin upon the matter to his father during the morning's walk. His father would be full of wrath; - but the wrath would have to be endured sooner or later.

Chapter 13

On the next morning Michel Voss and his son met in the kitchen, and found Marie already there. 'Well, my girl,' said Michel, as he patted Marie's shoulder, and kissed her forehead, 'you've been up getting a rare breakfast for these fellows, I see.' Marie smiled, and made some good-humoured reply. No one could have told by her face that there was anything amiss with her. 'It's the last favour of the kind he'll ever have at your hands,' continued Michel, 'and yet he doesn't seem to be half grateful.' George stood with his back to the kitchen fire, and did not say a word. It was impossible for him even to appear to be pleasant when such things were being said. Marie was a better hypocrite, and, though she said little, was able to look as though she could sympathise with her uncle's pleasant mirth. The two men had soon eaten their breakfast and were gone, and then Marie was left alone with her thoughts. Would George say anything to his father of what had passed up-stairs on the previous evening?

The two men started, and when they were alone together, and as long as Michel abstained from talking about Marie and her prospects, George was able to converse freely with his father. When they left the house the morning was just dawning, and the air was fresh and sharp. 'We shall soon have the frost here now,' said Michel, 'and then there will be no more grass for the cattle.'

'I suppose they can have them out on the low lands till the end of November. They always used.'

'Yes; they can have them out; but having them out and having food for them are different things. The people here have so much stock now, that directly the growth is checked by the frost, the land becomes almost bare. They forget the old saying - "Half stocking, whole profits; whole stocking, half profits!" And then, too, I think the winters are earlier here than they used to be. They'll have to go back to the Swiss plan, I fancy, and carry the food to the cattle in their houses. It may be old-fashioned, as they say; but I doubt whether the fodder does not go farther so.' Then as they began to ascend the mountain, he got on to the subject of his own business and George's prospects. 'The dues to the Commune are so heavy,' he said, 'that in fact there is little or nothing to be made out of the timber. It looks like a business, because many men are employed, and it's a kind of thing that spreads itself, and bears looking at. But it leaves nothing behind.'

'It's not quite so bad as that, I hope,' said George.

'Upon my word then it is not much better, my boy. When you've charged yourself with interest on the money spent on the mills, there is not much to boast about. You're bound to replant every yard you strip, and yet the Commune expects as high a rent as when there was no planting to be done at all. They couldn't get it, only that men like myself have their money in the mills, and can't well get out of the trade.'

'I don't think you'd like to give it up, father.'

'Well, no. It gives me exercise and something to do. The women manage most of it down at the house; but there must be a change when Marie has gone. I have hardly looked it in the face yet, but I know there must be a change. She has grown up among it till she has it all at her fingers' ends. I tell you what, George, she is a girl in a hundred, - a girl in a hundred. She is going to marry a rich man, and so it don't much signify; but if she married a poor man, she would be as good as a fortune to him. She'd make a fortune for any man. That's my belief. There is nothing she doesn't know, and nothing she doesn't understand.'

Why did his father tell him all this? George thought of the day on which his father had, as he was accustomed to say to himself, turned him out of the house because he wanted to marry this girl who was 'as good as a fortune' to any man. Had he, then, been imprudent in allowing himself to love such a girl? Could there be any good reason why his father should have wished that a 'fortune,' in every way so desirable, should go out of the family? 'She'll have nothing to do of that sort if she goes to Basle,' said George moodily.

'That is more than you can say,' replied his father. 'A woman married to a man of business can always find her share in it if she pleases. And with such a one as Adrian Urmand her side of the house will not be the least considerable.'

'I suppose he is little better than a fool,' said George.

'A fool! He is not a fool at all. If you were to see him buying, you would not call him a fool. He is very far from a fool.'

'It may be so. I do not know much of him myself.'

'You should not be so prone to think men fools till you find them so; especially those who are to be so near to yourself. No; - he's not a fool by any means. But he will know that he has got a clever wife, and he will not be ashamed to make use of her.'

George was unwilling to contradict his father at the present moment, as he had all but made up his mind to tell the whole story about himself and Marie before he returned to the house. He had not the slightest idea that by doing so he would be able to soften his father's heart. He was sure, on the contrary, that were he to do so, he and his father would go back to the hotel as enemies. But he was quite resolved that the story should be told sooner or later, - should be told before the day fixed for the wedding. If it was to be told by himself, what occasion could be so fitting as the present? But, if it were to be done on this morning, it would be unwise to harass his father by any small previous contradictions.

They were now up among the scattered prostrate logs, and had again taken up the question of the business of wood-cutting. 'No, George; it would never have done for you; not as a mainstay. I thought of giving it up to you once, but I knew that it would make a poor man of you.'

'I wish you had,' said George, who was unable to repress the feeling of his heart.

'Why do you say that? What a fool you must be if you think it! There is nothing you may not do where you are, and you have got it all into your own hands, with little or no outlay. The rent is nothing; and the business is there ready made for you. In your position, if you find the hotel is not enough, there is nothing you cannot take up.' They had now seated themselves on the trunk of a pine tree; and Michel Voss having drawn a pipe from his pocket and filled it, was lighting it as he sat upon the wood. 'No, my boy,' he continued, 'you'll have a better life of it than your father, I don't doubt. After all, the towns are better than the country. There is more to be seen and more to be learned. I don't complain. The Lord has been very good to me. I've had enough of everything, and have been able to keep my head up. But I feel a little sad when I look forward. You and Marie will both be gone; and your stepmother's friend, M. le Curé Gondin, does not make much society for me. I sometimes think, when I am smoking a pipe up here all alone, that this is the best of it all; - it will be when Marie has gone.' If his father thus thought of it, why did he send Marie away? If he thus thought of it, why had he sent his son away? Had it not already been within his power to keep both of them there together under his roof-tree? He had insisted on dividing them, and dismissing them from Granpere, one in one direction, and the other in another; - and then he complained of being alone! Surely his father was altogether unreasonable. 'And now one can't even get tobacco that is worth smoking,' continued Michel, in a melancholy tone. 'There used to be good tobacco, but I don't know where it has all gone.'

'I can send you over a little prime tobacco from Colmar, father.'

'I wish you would, George. This is foul stuff. But I sometimes think I'll give it up. What's the use of it? A man sits and smokes and smokes, and nothing comes of it. It don't feed him, nor clothe him, and it leaves nothing behind, - except a stink.'

'You're a little down in the mouth, father, or you wouldn't talk of giving up smoking.'

'I am down in the mouth, - terribly down in the mouth. Till it was all settled, I did not know how much I should feel Marie's going. Of course it had to be, but it makes an old man of me. There will be nothing left. Of course there's your stepmother, - as good a woman as ever lived, - and the children; but Marie was somehow the soul of us all. Give us another light, George. I'm blessed if I can keep the fire in the pipe at all.'

'And this,' thought George, 'is in truth the state of my father's mind! There are three of us concerned who are all equally dear to each other, my father, myself, and Marie Bromar. There is not one of them who doesn't feel that the presence of the others is necessary to his happiness. Here is my father declaring that the world will no longer have any savour for him because I am away in one place, and Marie is to be away in another. There is not the slightest real reason on earth why we should have been separated. Yet he, - he alone has done it; and we, - we are to break our hearts over it! Or rather he has not done it. He is about to do it. The sacrifice is not yet made, and yet it must be made, because my father is so unreasonable that no one will dare to point out to him where lies the way to his own happiness and to the happiness of those he loves!' It was thus that George Voss thought of it as he listened to his father's wailings.

But he himself, though he was hot in temper, was slow, or at least deliberate, in action. He did not even now speak out at once. When his father's pipe was finished he suggested that they should go on to a certain run for the fir-logs, which he himself - George Voss - had made - a steep grooved inclined plane by which the timber when cut in these parts could be sent down with a rush to the close neighbourhood of the sawmill below. They went and inspected the slide, and discussed the question of putting new wood into the groove. Michel, with the melancholy tone that had prevailed with him all the morning, spoke of matters as though any money spent in mending would be thrown away. There are moments in the lives of most of us in which it seems to us that there will never be more cakes and ale. George, however, talked of the children, and reminded his father that in matters of business nothing is so ruinous as ruin. 'If you've got to get your money out of a thing, it should always be in working order,' he said. Michel acknowledged the truth of the rule, but again declared that there was no money to be got out of the thing. He yielded, however, and promised that the repairs should be made. Then they went down to the mill, which was going at that time. George, as he stood by and watched the man and boy adjusting the logs to the cradle, and listened to the apparently self-acting saw as it did its work, and observed the perfection of the simple machinery which he himself had adjusted, and smelt the sweet scent of the newly-made sawdust, and listened to the music of the little stream, when, between whiles, the rattle of the mill would cease for half a minute, - George, as he stood in silence, looking at all this, listening to the sounds, smelling the perfume, thinking how much sweeter it all was than the little room in which Madame Faragon sat at Colmar, and in which it was, at any rate for the present, his duty to submit his accounts to her, from time to time, - resolved that he would at once make an effort. He knew his father's temper well. Might it not be that though there should be a quarrel for a time, everything would come right at last? As for Adrian Urmand, George did not believe, - or told himself that he did not believe, - that such a cur as he would suffer much because his hopes of a bride were not fulfilled.

They stayed for an hour at the saw-mill, and Michel, in spite of all that he had said about tobacco, smoked another pipe. While they were there, George, though his mind was full of other matter, continued to give his father practical advice about the business - how a new wheel should be supplied here, and a lately invented improvement introduced there. Each of them at the moment was care-laden with special thoughts of his own, but nevertheless, as men of business, they knew that the hour was precious and used it. To saunter into the woods and do nothing was not at all in accordance with Michel's usual mode of life; and though he hummed and hawed, and doubted and grumbled, he took a note of all his son said, and was quite of a mind to make use of his son's wit.

'I shall be over at Epinal the day after tomorrow,' he said as they left the mill, 'and I'll see if I can get the new crank there.'

'They'll be sure to have it at Heinman's,' said George, as they began to descend the hill. From the spot on which they had been standing the walk down to Granpere would take them more than an hour. It might well be that they might make it an affair of two or three hours, if they went up to other timber-cuttings on their route; but George was sure that as soon as he began to tell his story his father would make his way straight for home. He would be too much moved to think of his timber, and too angry to desire to remain a minute longer than he could help in company with his son. Looking at all the circumstances as carefully as he could, George thought that he had better begin at once. 'As you feel Marie's going so much,' he said, 'I wonder that you are so anxious to send her away.'

'That's a poor argument, George, and one that I should not have expected from you. Am I to keep her here all her life, doing no good for herself, simply because I like to have her here?

It is in the course of things that she should be married, and it is my duty to see that she marries well.'

'That is quite true, father.'

'Then why do you talk to me about sending her away? I don't send her away. Urmand comes and takes her away. I did the same when I was young. Now I'm old, and I have to be left behind. It's the way of nature.'

'But she doesn't want to be taken away,' said George, rushing at once at his subject.

'What do you mean by that?'

'Just what I say, father. She consents to be taken away, but she does not wish it.'

'I don't know what you mean. Has she been talking to you? Has she been complaining?'

'I have been talking to her. I came over from Colmar when I heard of this marriage on purpose that I might talk to her. I had at any rate a right to do that.'

'Right to do what? I don't know that you have any right. If you have been trying to do mischief in my house, George, I will never forgive you - never.'

'I will tell you the whole truth, father; and then you shall say yourself whether I have been trying to do mischief, and shall say also whether you will forgive me. You will remember when you told me that I was not to think of Marie Bromar for myself.'

'I do remember.'

'Well; I had thought of her. If you wanted to prevent that, you were too late.'

'You were boys and girls together; that is all.'

'Let me tell my story, father, and then you shall judge. Before you had spoken to me at all, Marie had given me her troth.'

'Nonsense!'

'Let me at least tell my story. She had done so, and I had given her mine; and when you told me to go, I went, not quite knowing then what it might be best that we should do, but feeling very sure that she would at least be true to me.'

'Truth to any such folly as that would be very wicked.'

'At any rate, I did nothing. I remained there month after month; meaning to do something when this was settled, - meaning to do something when that was settled; and then there came a sort of rumour to me that Marie was to be

Urmand's wife. I did not believe it, but I thought that I would come and see.'

'It was true.'

'No; - it was not true then. I came over, and was very angry because she was cold to me. She would not promise that there should be no such engagement; but there was none then. You see I will tell you everything as it occurred.'

'She is at any rate engaged to Adrian Urmand now, and for all our sakes you are bound not to interfere.'

'But yet I must tell my story. I went back to Colmar, and then, after a while, there came tidings, true tidings, that she was engaged to this man. I came over again yesterday, determined, - you may blame me if you will, father, but listen to me, - determined to throw her falsehood in her teeth.'

'Then I will protect her from you,' said Michel Voss, turning upon his son as though he meant to strike him with his staff.

'Ah, father,' said George, pausing and standing opposite to the innkeeper, 'but who is to protect her from you? If I had found that that which you are doing was making her happy, - I would have spoken my mind indeed; I would have shown her once, and once only, what she had done to me; how she had destroyed me, - and then I would have gone, and troubled none of you any more.'

'You had better go now, and bring us no more trouble. You are all trouble.'

'But her worst trouble will still cling to her. I have found that it is so. She has taken this man not because she loves him, but because you have bidden her.'

'She has taken him, and she shall marry him.'

'I cannot say that she has been right, father; but she deserves no such punishment as that. Would you make her a wretched woman for ever, because she has done wrong in striving to obey you?'

'She has not done wrong in striving to obey me. She has done right. I do not believe a word of this.'

'You can ask her yourself.'

'I will ask her nothing, - except that she shall not speak to you any farther about it. You have come here wilfully-minded to disturb us all.'

'Father, that is unjust.'

'I say it is true. She was contented and happy before you came. She loves the man, and is ready to marry him on the day fixed. Of course she will marry him. You would not have us go back from our word now?'

'Certainly I would. If he be a man, and she tells him that she repents, - if she tells him all the truth, of course he will give her back her troth. I would do so to any woman that only hinted that she wished it.'

'No such hint shall be given. I will hear nothing of it. I shall not speak to Marie on the subject, - except to desire her to have no farther converse with you. Nor will I speak of it again to yourself; unless you wish me to bid you go from me altogether, you will not mention the matter again.' So saying, Michel Voss strode on, and would not even turn his eyes in the direction of his son. He strode on, making his way down the hill at the fastest pace that he could achieve, every now and then raising his hat and wiping the perspiration from his brow. Though he had spoken of Marie's departure as a loss that would be very hard to bear, the very idea that anything should be allowed to interfere with the marriage which he had planned was unendurable. What; - after all that had been said and done, consent that there should be no marriage between his niece and the rich young merchant! Never. He did not stop for a moment to think how much of truth there might be in his son's statement. He would not even allow himself to remember that he had forced Adrian Urmand as a suitor upon his niece. He had had his qualms of conscience upon that matter, - and it was possible that they might return to him. But he would not stop now to look at that side of the question. The young people were betrothed. The marriage was a thing settled, and it should be celebrated. He had never broken his faith to any man, and he would not break it to Adrian Urmand. He strode on down the mountain, and there was not a word more said between him and his son till they reached the inn doors. 'You understand me,' he said then. 'Not a word more to Marie.' After that he went up at once to his wife's chamber, and desired that Marie might be sent to him there. During his rapid walk home he had made up his mind as to what he would do. He would not be severe to his niece. He would simply ask her one question.

'My dear,' he said, striving to be calm, but telling her by his countenance as plainly as words could have done all that had passed between him and his son, - 'Marie, my dear, I take it for - granted - there is nothing to - to - to interrupt our plans.'

'In what way, uncle?' she asked, merely wanting to gain a moment for thought.

'In any way. In no way. Just say that there is nothing wrong, and that will be sufficient.' She stood silent, not having a word to say to him. 'You know what I mean, Marie. You intend to marry Adrian Urmand?'

'I suppose so,' said Marie in a low whisper.

'Look here, Marie, - if there be any doubt about it, we will part, - and for ever. You shall never look upon my face again. My honour is pledged, - and yours.' Then he hurried out of the room, down into the kitchen, and without staying there a moment went out into the yard, and walked through to the stables. His passion had been so strong and uncontrollable, that he had been unable to remain with his niece and exact a promise from her.

George, when he saw his father go through to the stables, entered the house. He had already made up his mind that he would return at once to Colmar, without waiting to have more angry words. Such words would serve him not at all. But he must if possible see Marie, and he must also tell his stepmother that he was about to depart. He found them both together, and at once, very abruptly, declared that he was to start immediately.

'You have quarrelled with your father, George,' said Madame Voss.

'I hope not. I hope that he has not quarrelled with me. But it is better that I should go.'

'What is it, George? I hope it is nothing serious.' Madame Voss as she said this looked at Marie, but Marie had turned her face away. George also looked at her, but could not see her countenance. He did not dare to ask her to give him an interview alone; nor had he quite determined what he would say to her if they were together. 'Marie,' said Madame Voss, 'do you know what this is about?'

'I wish I had died,' said Marie, 'before I had come into this house. I have made hatred and bitterness between those who

113

should love each other better than all the world!' Then Madame Voss was able to guess what had been the cause of the quarrel.

'Marie,' said George very slowly, 'if you will only ask your own heart what you ought to do, and be true to what it tells you, there is no reason even yet that you should be sorry that you came to Granpere. But if you marry a man whom you do not love, you will sin against him, and against me, and against yourself, and against God!' Then he took up his hat and went out.

In the courtyard he met his father.

'Where are you going now, George?' said his father.

'To Colmar. It is better that I should go at once. Good-bye, father;' and he offered his hand to his parent.

'Have you spoken to Marie?'

'My mother will tell you what I have said. I have spoken nothing in private.'

'Have you said anything about her marriage?'

'Yes. I have told her that she could not honestly marry the man she did not love.'

'What right have you, sir,' said Michel, nearly choked with wrath, 'to interfere in the affairs of my household? You had better go, and go at once. If you return again before they are married, I will tell the servants to put you off the place!' George Voss made no answer, but having found his horse and his gig, drove himself off to Colmar.

Chapter 14

George Voss, as he drove back to Colmar and thought of what had been done during the last twenty-four hours, did not find that he had much occasion for triumph. He had, indeed, the consolation of knowing that the girl loved him, and in that there was a certain amount of comfort. As he had ever been thinking about her since he had left Granpere, so also had she been thinking of him. His father had told him that they had been no more than children when they parted, and had ridiculed the idea that any affection formed so long back and at so early an age should have lasted. But it had lasted; and was now as strong in Marie's breast as it was in his own. He had learned this at any rate by his journey to Granpere, and there was something of consolation in the knowledge. But, nevertheless, he did not find that he could triumph. Marie had been weak enough to yield to his father once, and would yield to him, he thought, yet again. Women in this respect - as he told himself - were different from men. They were taught by the whole tenor of their lives to submit, - unless they could conquer by underhand unseen means, by little arts, by coaxing, and by tears. Marie, he did not doubt, had tried all these, and had failed. His father's purpose had been too strong for her, and she had yielded. Having submitted once, of course she would submit again. There was about his father a spirit of masterfulness, which he was sure Marie would not be able to withstand. And then there would be - strong against his interests, George thought - that feeling so natural to a woman, that as all the world had been told of her coming marriage, she would be bound to go through with it. The idea of it had become familiar to her. She had conquered the repugnance which she must at first have felt, and had made herself accustomed to regard this man as her future husband. And then there would be Madame Voss against him, and M. le Curé, - both of whom would think it infinitely better for Marie's future welfare, that she should marry a Roman Catholic, as was Urmand, than a Protestant such as was he, George Voss. And then the money! Even if he could bring himself to believe that the money was nothing to Marie, it would be so much to all those by whom Marie would be surrounded, that it would be impossible that she should be preserved from its influence.

It is not often that young people really know each other; but George certainly did not know Marie Bromar. In the first place, though he had learned from her the secret of her heart, he had not taught himself to understand how his own sullen silence had acted upon her. He knew now that she had continued to love him; but he did not know how natural it had been that she should have believed that he had forgotten her. He could not, therefore, understand how different must now be her feelings in reference to this marriage with Adrian, from what they had been when she had believed herself to be utterly deserted. And then he did not comprehend how thoroughly unselfish she had been; - how she had struggled to do her duty to others, let the cost be what it might to herself. She had plighted herself to Adrian Urmand, not because there had seemed to her to be any brightness in the prospect which such a future promised to her, but because she did verily believe that, circumstanced as she was, it would be better that she should submit herself to her friends. All this George Voss did not understand. He had thrown his thunderbolt, and had seen that it had been efficacious. Its efficacy had been such that his wrath had been turned into tenderness. He had been so changed in his purpose, that he had been induced to make an appeal to his father at the cost of his father's enmity. But that appeal had been in vain, and, as he thought of it all, he told himself that on the appointed day Marie Bromar would become the wife of Adrian Urmand. He knew well enough that a girl betrothed is a girl already half married.

He was very wretched as he drove his horse along. Though there was a solace in the thought that the memory of him had still remained in Marie's heart, there was a feeling akin to despair in this also. His very tenderness towards her was more unendurable than would have been his wrath. The pity of it! The pity of it! It was that which made him sore of heart and faint of spirit. If he could have reproached her as cold, mercenary, unworthy, heartless, even though he had still loved her, he could have supported himself by his anger against her unworthiness. But as it was there was no such support for him. Though she had been in fault, her virtue towards him was greater than her fault. She still loved him. She still loved him, - though she could not be his wife.

Then he thought of Adrian Urmand and of the man's success and wealth, and general prosperity in the world. What if he should go over to Basle and take Adrian Urmand by the throat and choke him? What if he should at least half choke the successful man, and make it well understood that the other half would come unless the successful man would consent to relinquish his bride? George, though he did not expect success for himself, was fully purposed that Urmand should not succeed without some interference from him, - by means of choking or otherwise. He would find some way of making himself disagreeable. If it were only by speaking his mind, he thought that he could speak it in such a way that the Basle merchant would not like it. He would tell Urmand in the first place that Marie was won not at all by affection, not in the least by any personal regard for her suitor, but altogether by a feeling of duty towards her uncle. And he would point out to this suitor how dastardly a thing it would be to take advantage of a girl so placed. He planned a speech or two as he drove along which he thought that even Urmand, thick-skinned as he believed him to be, would dislike to hear. 'You may have her, perhaps,' he would say to him, 'as so much goods that you would buy, because she is, as a thing in her uncle's hands, to be bought. She believes it to be her duty, as being altogether dependent, to be disposed of as her uncle may choose. And she will go to you, as she would to any other man who might make the purchase. But as for loving you, you don't even believe that she loves you. She will keep your house for you; but she will never love you. She will keep your house for you, - unless, indeed, she should find you to be so intolerable to her, that she should be forced to leave you. It is in that way that you will have her, - if you are so low a thing as to be willing to take her so.' He planned various speeches of such a nature - not intending to trust entirely to speeches, but to proceed to some attempt at choking afterwards if it should be necessary. Marie Bromar should not become Adrian Urmand's wife without some effort on his part. So resolving, he drove into the yard of the hotel at Colmar.

As soon as he entered the house Madame Faragon began to ask him questions about the wedding. When was it to be? George thought for a moment, and then remembered that he had not even heard the day named.

'Why don't you answer me, George?' said the old woman angrily. 'You must know when it's going to be.'

'I don't know that it's going to be at all,' said George.

'Not going to be at all! Why not? There is not anything wrong, is there? Were they not betrothed? Why don't you tell me, George?'

'Yes; they were betrothed.'

'And is he crying off? I should have thought Michel Voss was the man to strangle him if he did that.'

'And I am the man to strangle him if he don't,' said George, walking out of the room.

He knew that he had been silly and absurd, but he knew also that he was so moved as to have hardly any control over himself. In the few words that he had now said to Madame Faragon he had, as he felt, told the story of his own disappointment; and yet he had not in the least intended to take the old woman into his confidence. He had not meant to have said a word about the quarrel between himself and his father, and now he had told everything.

When she saw him again in the evening, of course she asked him some farther questions.

'George,' she said, 'I am afraid things are not going pleasantly at Granpere.'

'Not altogether,' he answered.

'But I suppose the marriage will go on?' To this he made no answer, but shook his head, showing how impatient he was at being thus questioned. 'You ought to tell me,' said Madame Faragon plaintively, 'considering how interested I must be in all that concerns you.'

'I have nothing to tell.'

'But is the marriage to be put off?' again demanded Madame Faragon, with extreme anxiety.

118

'Not that I know of, Madame Faragon: they will not ask me whether it is to be put off or not.'

'But have they quarrelled with M. Urmand?'

'No; nobody has quarrelled with M. Urmand.'

'Was he there, George?'

'What, with me! No; he was not there with me. I have never seen the man since I first left Granpere to come here.' And then George Voss began to think what might have happened had Adrian Urmand been at the hotel while he was there himself. After all, what could he have said to Adrian Urmand? or what could he have done to him?

'He hasn't written, has he, to say that he is off his bargain?' Poor Madame Faragon was almost pathetic in her anxiety to learn what had really occurred at the Lion d'Or.

'Certainly not. He has not written at all.'

'Then what is it, George?'

'I suppose it is this, - that Marie Bromar cares nothing for him.'

'But so rich as he is! And they say, too, such a good-looking young man.'

'It is wonderful, is it not? It is next to a miracle that there should be a girl deaf and blind to such charms. But, nevertheless, I believe it is so. They will probably make her marry him, whether she likes it or not.'

'But she is betrothed to him. Of course she will marry him.'

'Then there will be an end of it,' said George.

There was one other question which Madame Faragon longed to ask; but she was almost too much afraid of her young friend to put it into words. At last she plucked up courage, and did ask her question after an ambiguous way.

'But I suppose it is nothing to you, George?'

'Nothing at all. Nothing on earth,' said he. 'How should it be anything to me?' Then he hesitated for a while, pausing to think whether or not he would tell the truth to Madame Faragon. He knew that there was no one on earth, setting aside his father and Marie Bromar, to whom he was really so dear as he was to this old woman. She would probably do more for him, if it might possibly be in her power to do anything, than any other of his friends. And, moreover, he did not like the idea of being false to her, even on such a subject as this. 'It is only this to me,' he said, 'that she had promised to be my wife, before they had ever mentioned Urmand's name to her.'

'O, George!'

'And why should she not have promised?'

'But, George; - during all this time you have never mentioned it.'

'There are some things, Madame Faragon, which one doesn't mention. And I do not know why I should have mentioned it at all. But you understand all about it now. Of course she will marry the man. It is not likely that my father should fail to have his own way with a girl who is dependent on him.'

'But he - M. Urmand; he would give her up if he knew it all, would he not?'

To this George made no instant answer; but the idea was there, in his mind - that the linen merchant might perhaps be induced to abandon his purpose, if he could be made to understand that Marie wished it. 'If he have any touch of manhood about him he would do so,' said he.

'And what will you do, George?'

'Do! I shall do nothing. What should I do? My father has turned me out of the house. That is the whole of it. I do not know that there is anything to be done.' Then he went out, and there was nothing more said upon the question. For the next three or four days there was nothing said. As he went in and out Madame Faragon would look at him with anxious eyes, questioning herself how far such a feeling of love might in truth make this young man forlorn and wretched. As far as she could judge by his manner he was very forlorn and very wretched. He did his work indeed, and was busy about the place, as was his wont. But there was a look of pain in his face, which made her old heart grieve, and by degrees her good wishes for the object, which seemed to be so much to him, became eager and hot.

'Is there nothing to be done?' she asked at last, putting out her fat hand to take hold of his in sympathy.

'There is nothing to be done,' said George, who, however, hated himself because he was doing nothing, and still thought occasionally of that plan of choking his rival.

'If you were to go to Basle and see the man?'

'What could I say to him, if I did see him? After all, it is not him that I can blame. I have no just ground of quarrel with him. He has done nothing that is not fair. Why should he not love her if it suits him? Unless he were to fight me, indeed - '

'O, George! let there be no fighting.'

'It would do no good, I fear.'

'None, none, none,' said she.

'If I were to kill him, she could not be my wife then.'

'No, no; certainly not.'

'And if I wounded him, it would make her like him perhaps. If he were to kill me, indeed, there might be some comfort in that.'

After this Madame Faragon made no farther suggestions that her young friend should go to Basle.

Chapter 15

During the remainder of the day on which George had left Granpere, the hours did not fly very pleasantly at the Lion d'Or. Michel Voss had gone to his niece immediately upon his return from his walk, intending to obtain a renewed pledge from her that she would be true to her engagement. But he had been so full of passion, so beside himself with excitement, so disturbed by all that he had heard, that he had hardly waited with Marie long enough to obtain such pledge, or to learn from her that she refused to give it. He had only been able to tell her that if she hesitated about marrying Adrian she should never look upon his face again; and then without staying for a reply he had left her. He had been in such a tremor of passion that he had been unable to demand an answer. After that, when George was gone, he kept away from her during the remainder of the morning. Once or twice he said a few words to his wife, and she counselled him to take no farther outward notice of anything that George had said to him. 'It will all come right if you will only be a little calm with her,' Madame Voss had said. He had tossed his head and declared that he was calm; - the calmest man in all Lorraine. Then he had come to his wife again, and she had again given him some good practical advice. 'Don't put it into her head that there is to be a doubt,' said Madame Voss.

'I haven't put it into her head,' he answered angrily.

'No, my dear, no; but do not allow her to suppose that anybody else can put it there either. Let the matter go on. She will see the things bought for her wedding, and when she remembers that she has allowed them to come into the house without remonstrating, she will be quite unable to object. Don't give her an opportunity of objecting.' Michel Voss again shook his head, as though his wife were an unreasonable woman, and swore that it was not he who had given Marie such opportunity. But he made up his mind to do as his wife recommended. 'Speak softly to her, my dear,' said Madame Voss.

'Don't I always speak softly?' said he, turning sharply round upon his spouse.

He made his attempt to speak softly when he met Marie about the house just before supper. He put his hand upon her shoulder, and smiled, and murmured some word of love. He was by no means crafty in what he did. Craft indeed was not the strong point of his character. She took his rough hand and kissed it, and looked up lovingly, beseechingly into his face. She knew that he was asking her to consent to the sacrifice, and he knew that she was imploring him to spare her. This was not what Madame Voss had meant by speaking softly. Could she have been allowed to dilate upon her own convictions, or had she been able adequately to express her own ideas, she would have begged that there might be no sentiment, no romance, no kissing of hands, no looking into each other's faces, - no half-murmured tones of love. Madame Voss believed strongly that the every-day work of the world was done better without any of these glancings and glimmerings of moonshine. But then her husband was, by nature, of a fervid temperament, given to the influence of unexpressed poetic emotions; - and thus subject, in spite of the strength of his will, to much weakness of purpose. Madame Voss perhaps condemned her husband in this matter the more because his romantic disposition never showed itself in his intercourse with her. He would kiss Marie's hand, and press Marie's wrist, and hold dialogues by the eye with Marie. But with his wife his speech was, - not exactly yea, yea, and nay, nay, - but yes, yes, and no, no. It was not unnatural therefore that she should specially dislike this weakness of his which came from his emotional temperament.

'I would just let things go, as though there were nothing special at all,' she said again to him, before supper, in a whisper.

'And so I do. What would you have me say?'

'Don't mind petting her, but just be as you would be any other day.'

'I am as I would be any other day,' he replied. However, he knew that his wife was right, and was in a certain way aware that if he could only change himself and be another sort of man, he might manage the matter better. He could be fiercely angry, or caressingly affectionate. But he was unable to adopt that safe and golden mean, which his wife recommended. He could not keep himself from interchanging a piteous glance or two with Marie at supper, and put a great deal too much unction into his caress to please Madame Voss, when Marie came to kiss him before she went to bed.

In the mean time Marie was quite aware that it was incumbent on her to determine what she would do. It may be as well to declare at once that she had determined - had determined fully, before her uncle and George had started for their walk up to the wood-cutting. When she was giving them their breakfast that morning her mind was fully made up. She had had the night to lie awake upon it, to think it over, and to realise all that George had told her. It had come to her as quite a new thing that the man whom she worshipped, worshipped her too. While she believed that nobody else loved her; - when she could tell herself that her fate was nothing to anybody; - as long as it had seemed to her that the world for her must be cold, and hard, and material; - so long could she reconcile to herself, after some painful, dubious fashion, the idea of being the wife either of Adrian Urmand, or of any other man. Some kind of servitude was needful, and if her uncle was decided that she must be banished from his house, the kind of servitude which was proposed to her at Basle would do as well as another. But when she had learned the truth, - a truth so unexpected, - then such servitude became impossible to her. On that morning, when she came down to give the men their breakfast, she had quite determined that let the consequences be what they might she would never become the wife of Adrian Urmand. Madame Voss had told her husband that when Marie saw the things purchased for her wedding coming into the house, the very feeling that the goods had been bought would bind her to her engagement. Marie had thought of that also, and was aware that she must lose no time in making her purpose known, so that articles which would be unnecessary might not be purchased. On that very morning, while the men had been up in the mountain, she had sat with her aunt hemming sheets; - intended as an addition to the already overflowing stock possessed by M. Urmand. It was with difficulty that she had brought herself to do that, - telling herself, however, that as the linen was there, it must be hemmed; when there had come a question of marking the sheets, she had evaded the task, - not without raising suspicion in the bosom of Madame Voss.

But it was, as she knew, absolutely necessary that her uncle should be informed of her purpose. When he had come to her after the walk, and demanded of her whether she still intended to marry Adrian Urmand, she had answered him falsely. 'I suppose so,' she had said. The question - such a question as it was - had been put to her too abruptly to admit of a true answer on the spur of the moment. But the falsehood almost stuck in her throat and was a misery to her till she could set it right by a clear declaration of the truth. She had yet to determine what she would do; - how she would tell this truth; in what way she would insure to herself the power of carrying out her purpose. Her mind, the reader must remember, was somewhat dark in the matter. She was betrothed to the man, and she had always heard that a betrothal was half a marriage. And yet she knew of instances in which marriages had been broken off after betrothal quite as ceremonious as her own - had been broken off without scandal or special censure from the Church. Her aunt, indeed, and M. le Curé had, ever since the plighting of her troth to M. Urmand, spoken of the matter in her presence, as though the wedding were a thing already nearly done; - not suggesting by the tenor of their speech that any one could wish in any case to make a change, but pointing out incidentally that any change was now out of the question. But Marie had been sharp enough to understand perfectly the gist of her aunt's manoeuvres and of the priest's incidental information. The thing could be done, she know; and she feared no one in the doing of it, - except her uncle. But she did fear that if she simply told him that it must be done, he would have such a power over her that she would not succeed. In what way could she do it first, and then tell him afterwards?

At last she determined that she would write a letter to M. Urmand, and show a copy of the letter to her uncle when the post should have taken it so far out of Granpere on its way to Basle, as to make it impossible that her uncle should recall it. Much of the day after George's departure, and much of the night, was spent in the preparation of this letter. Marie Bromar was not so well practised in the writing of letters as will be the majority of the young ladies who may, perhaps, read her history. It was a difficult thing for her to begin the letter, and a difficult thing for her to bring it to its end. But the letter was written and sent. The post left Granpere at about eight in the morning, taking all letters by way of Remiremont; and on the day following George's departure, the post took Marie Bromar's letter to M. Urmand.

When it was gone, her state of mind was very painful. Then it was necessary that she should show the copy to her uncle. She had posted the letter between six and seven with her own hands, and had then come trembling back to the inn, fearful that her uncle should discover what she had done before her letter should be beyond his reach. When she saw the mail conveyance go by on its route to Remiremont, then she knew that she must begin to prepare for her uncle's wrath. She thought that she had heard that the letters were detained some time at Remiremont before they went on to Epinal in one direction, and to Mulhouse in the other. She looked at the railway time-table which was hung up in one of the passages of the inn, and saw the hour of the departure of the diligence from Remiremont to catch the train at Mulhouse for Basle. When that hour was passed, the conveyance of her letter was insured, and then she must show the copy to her uncle. He came into the house about twelve, and eat his dinner with his wife in the little chamber. Marie, who was in and out of the room during the time, would not sit down with them. When pressed to do so by her uncle, she declared that she had eaten lately and was not hungry. It was seldom that she would sit down to dinner, and this therefore gave rise to no special remark. As soon as his meal was over, Michel Voss got up to go out about his business, as was usual with him. Then Marie followed him into the passage. 'Uncle Michel,' she said, 'I want to speak to you for a moment; will you come with me?'

'What is it about, Marie?'

'If you will come, I will show you.'

'Show me! What will you show me?'

'It's a letter, Uncle Michel. Come up-stairs and you shall see it.' Then he followed her up-stairs, and in the long public room, which was at that hour deserted, she took out of her pocket the copy of her letter to Adrian Urmand, and put it into her uncle's hands. 'It is a letter, Uncle Michel, which I have written to M. Urmand. It went this morning, and you must see it.'

'A letter to Urmand,' he said, as he took the paper suspiciously into his hands.

'Yes, Uncle Michel. I was obliged to write it. It is the truth, and I was obliged to let him know it. I am afraid you will be angry with me, and - turn me away; but I cannot help it.'

The letter was as follows:

'The Hotel Lion d'Or, Granpere,
October 1, 186-.

'M. URMAND,

'I take up my pen in great sorrow and remorse to write you a letter, and to prevent you from coming over here for me, as you intended, on this day fortnight. I have promised to be your wife, but it cannot be. I know that I have behaved very badly, but it would be worse if I were to go on and deceive you. Before I knew you I had come to be fond of another man; and I find now, though I have struggled hard to do what my uncle wishes, that I could not promise to love you and be your wife. I have not told Uncle Michel yet, but I shall as soon as this letter is gone.

'I am very, very sorry for the trouble I have given you. I did not mean to be bad. I hope that you will forget me, and try to forgive me. No one knows better than I do how bad I have been.

'Your most humble servant,
'With the greatest respect,
'MARIE BROMAR.'

The letter had taken her long to write, and it took her uncle long to read, before he came to the end of it. He did not get through a line without sundry interruptions, which all arose from his determination to contradict at once every assertion which she made. 'You cannot prevent his coming,' he said, 'and it shall not be prevented.' 'Of course, you have promised to be his wife, and it must be.' 'Nonsense about deceiving him. He is not deceived at all.' 'Trash - you are not fond of another man. It is all nonsense.' 'You must do what your uncle wishes. You must, now! you must! Of course, you will love him. Why can't you let all that come as it does with others?' 'Letter gone; - yes indeed, and now I must go after it.' 'Trouble! - yes! Why could you not tell me before you sent it? Have I not always been good to you?' 'You have not been bad; not before. You have been very good. It is this that is bad.' 'Forget you indeed. Of course he won't. How should he? Are you not betrothed to him? He'll forgive you fast enough, when you just say that you did not know what you were about when you were writing it.' Thus her uncle went on; and as the outburst of his wrath was, as it were, chopped into little bits by his having to continue the reading of the letter, the storm did not fall upon Marie's head so violently as she had expected. 'There's a pretty kettle of fish you've made!' said he as soon as he had finished reading the letter. 'Of course, it means nothing.'

'But it must mean something, Uncle Michel.'

'I say it means nothing. Now I'll tell you what I shall do, Marie. I shall start for Basle directly. I shall get there by twelve o'clock to-night by going through Colmar, and I shall endeavour to intercept the letter before Urmand would receive it to-morrow.' This was a cruel blow to Marie after all her precautions. 'If I cannot do that, I shall at any rate see him before he gets it. That is what I shall do; and you must let me tell him, Marie, that you repent having written the letter.'

'But I don't repent it, Uncle Michel; I don't, indeed. I can't repent it. How can I repent it when I really mean it? I shall never become his wife; - indeed I shall not. O, Uncle Michel, pray, pray, pray do not go to Basle!'

But Michel Voss resolved that he would go to Basle, and to Basle he went. The immediate weight, too, of Marie's misery was aggravated by the fact that in order to catch the train for Basle at Colmar, her uncle need not start quite immediately. There was an hour during which he could continue to exercise his eloquence upon his niece, and endeavour to induce her to authorise him to contradict her own letter. He appealed first to her affection, and then to her duty; and after that, having failed in these appeals, he poured forth the full vials of his wrath upon her head. She was ungrateful, obstinate, false, unwomanly, disobedient, irreligious, sacrilegious, and an idiot. In the fury of his anger, there was hardly any epithet of severe rebuke which he spared, and yet, as every cruel word left his mouth, he assured her that it should all be taken to mean nothing, if she would only now tell him that he might nullify the letter. Though she had deserved all these bad things which he had spoken of her, yet she should be regarded as having deserved none of them, should again be accepted as having in all points done her duty, if she would only, even now, be obedient. But she was not to be shaken. She had at last formed a resolution, and her uncle's words had no effect towards turning her from it. 'Uncle Michel,' she said at last, speaking with much seriousness of purpose, and a dignity of person that was by no means thrown away upon him, 'if I am what you say, I had better go away from your house. I know I have been bad. I was bad to say that I would marry M. Urmand. I will not defend myself. But nothing on earth shall make me marry him. You had better let me go away, and get a place as a servant among our friends at Epinal.' But Michel Voss, though he was heaping abuse upon her with the hope that he might thus achieve his purpose, had not the remotest idea of severing the connection which bound him and her together. He wanted to do her good, not evil. She was exquisitely dear to him. If she would only let him have his way and provide for her welfare as he saw, in his wisdom, would be best, he would at once take her in his arms again and tell her that she was the apple of his eye. But she would not; and he went at last off on his road to Colmar and Basle, gnashing his teeth in anger.

Chapter 16

Nothing was said to Marie about her sins on that afternoon after her uncle had started on his journey. Everything in the hotel was blank, and sad, and gloomy; but there was, at any rate, the negative comfort of silence, and Marie was allowed to go about the house and do her work without rebuke. But she observed that the Curé - M. le Curé Gondin - sat much with her aunt during the evening, and she did not doubt but that she herself and her iniquities made the subject of their discourse.

M. le Curé Gondin, as he was generally called at Granpere, - being always so spoken of, with his full name and title, by the large Protestant portion of the community, - was a man very much respected by all the neighbourhood. He was respected by the Protestants because he never interfered with them, never told them, either behind their backs or before their faces, that they would be damned as heretics, and never tried the hopeless task of converting them. In his intercourse with them he dropped the subject of religion altogether, - as a philologist or an entomologist will drop his grammar or his insects in his intercourse with those to whom grammar and insects are matters of indifference. And he was respected by the Catholics of both sorts, - by those who did not and by those who did adhere with strictness to the letter of their laws of religion. With the former he did his duty, perhaps without much enthusiasm. He preached to them, if they would come and listen to him. He christened them, confessed them, and absolved them from their sins, - of course, after due penitence. But he lived with them, too, in a friendly way, pronouncing no anathemas against them, because they were not as attentive to their religious exercises as they might have been. But with those who took a comfort in sacred things, who liked to go to early masses in cold weather, to be punctual at ceremonies, to say the rosary as surely as the evening came, who knew and performed all the intricacies of fasting as ordered by the bishop, down to the refinement of an egg more or less, in the whole Lent, or the absence of butter from the day's cookery, - with these he had all that enthusiasm which such people like to encounter in their priest. We may say, therefore, that he was a wise man, - and probably, on the whole, a good man; that he did good service in his parish, and helped his people along in their lives not inefficiently. He was a small man, with dark hair very closely cut, with a tonsure that was visible but not more than visible; with a black beard that was shaved every Tuesday, Friday, and Saturday evenings, but which was very black indeed on the Tuesday and Friday mornings. He always wore the black gown of his office, but would go about his parish with an ordinary soft slouch hat, - thus subjecting his appearance to an absence of ecclesiastical trimness which, perhaps, the most enthusiastic of his friends regretted. Madame Voss certainly would have wished that he would have had himself shaved at any rate every other day, and that he would have abstained from showing himself in the streets of Granpere without his clerical hat. But, though she was very intimate with her Curé, and had conferred upon him much material kindness, she had never dared to express her opinion to him upon these matters.

During much of that afternoon M. le Curé sat with Madame Voss, but not a word was said to Marie about her disobedience either by him or by her. Nevertheless, Marie felt that her sins were being discussed, and that the lecture was coming. She herself had never quite liked M. le Curé - not having any special reason for disliking him, but regarding him as a man who was perhaps a little deficient in spirit, and perhaps a trifle too mindful of his creature comforts. M. le Curé took a great deal of snuff, and Marie did not like snuff taking. Her uncle smoked a great deal of tobacco, and that she thought very nice and proper in a man. Had her uncle taken the snuff and the priest smoked the tobacco, she would probably have equally approved of her uncle's practice and disapproved that of the priest; - because she loved the one and did not love the other. She had thought it probable that she might be sent for during the evening, and had, therefore, made for herself an immensity of household work, the performance of all which on that very evening the interests of the Lion d'Or would imperatively demand. The work was all done, but no message from Aunt Josey summoned Marie into the little parlour.

Nevertheless Marie had been quite right in her judgment. On the following morning, between eight and nine, M. le Curé was again in the house, and had a cup of coffee taken to him in the little parlour. Marie, who felt angry at his return, would not take it herself, but sent it in by the hands of Peter Veque. Peter Veque returned in a few minutes with a message to Marie, saying that M. le Curé wished to see her.

'Tell him that I am very busy,' said Marie. 'Say that uncle is away, and that there is a deal to do. Ask him if another day won't suit as well.'

She knew when she sent this message that another day would not suit as well. And she must have known also that her uncle's absence made no difference in her work. Peter came back with a request from Madame Voss that Marie would go to her at once. Marie pressed her lips together, clenched her fists, and walked down into the room without the delay of an instant.

'Marie, my dear,' said Madame Voss, 'M. le Curé wishes to speak to you. I will leave you for a few minutes.' There was nothing for it but to listen. Marie could not refuse to be lectured by the priest. But she told herself that having had the courage to resist her uncle, it certainly was out of the question that any one else should have the power to move her.

'My dear Marie,' began the Curé, 'your aunt has been telling me of this little difference between you and your affianced husband. Won't you sit down, Marie, because we shall be able so to talk more comfortably?'

'I don't want to talk about it at all,' said Marie. But she sat down as she was bidden.

'But, my dear, it is needful that your friends should talk to you. I am sure that you have too much sense to think that a young woman like yourself should refuse to hear her friends.' Marie had it almost on her tongue to tell the priest that the only friends to whom she chose to listen were her uncle and her aunt, but she thought that it might perhaps be better that she should remain silent. 'Of course, my dear, a young person like you must know that she must walk by advice, and I am sure you must feel that no one can give it you more fittingly than your own priest.' Then he took a large pinch of snuff.

'If it were anything to do with the Church, - yes,' she said.

'And this has to do with the Church, very much. Indeed I do not know how any of our duties in this life cannot have to do with the Church. There can be no duty omitted as to which you would not acknowledge that it was necessary that you should get absolution from your priest.'

'But that would be in the church,' said Marie, not quite knowing how to make good her point.

'Whether you are in the church or out of it, is just the same. If you were sick and in bed, would your priest be nothing to you then?'

'But I am quite well, Father Gondin.'

'Well in health; but sick in spirit, - as I am sure you must own. And I must explain to you, my dear, that this is a matter in which your religious duty is specially in question. You have been betrothed, you know, to M. Urmand.'

'But people betrothed are very often not married,' said Marie quickly. 'There was Annette Lolme at Saint Die. She was betrothed to Jean Stein at Pugnac. That was only last winter. And then there was something wrong about the money; and the betrothal went for nothing, and Father Carrier himself said it was all right. If it was all right for Annette Lolme, it must be all right for me as far as betrothing goes.'

The story that Marie told so clearly was perfectly true, and M. le Curé Gondin knew that it was true. He wished now to teach Marie that if certain circumstances should occur after a betrothal which would make the marriage inexpedient in the eyes of the parents of the young people, then the authority of the Church would not exert itself to insist on the sacred nature of the pledge; - but that if the pledge was to be called in question simply at the instance of a capricious young woman, then the Church would have full power. His object, in short, was to insist on parental authority, giving to parental authority some little additional strength from his own sacerdotal recognition of the sanctity of the betrothing promise. But he feared that Marie would be too strong for him, if not also too clear-headed.

'You cannot mean to tell me,' said he, 'that you think such a solemn promise as you have given to this young man, taking one from him as solemn in return, is to go for nothing?'

'I am very sorry that I promised, - very sorry indeed; but I cannot keep my promise.'

'You are bound to keep it, especially as all your friends wish the marriage, and think that it will be good for you. Annette Lolme's friends wished her not to marry. It is my duty to tell you, Marie, that if you break your faith to M. Urmand, you will commit a very grievous sin, and you will commit it with your eyes open.'

'If Annette Lolme might change her mind because her lover had not got as much money as people wanted, I am sure I may change mine because I don't love a man.'

'Annette did what her friends advised her.'

'Then a girl must always do what her friends tell her? If I don't marry M. Urmand, I sha'n't be wicked for breaking my promise, but for disobeying Uncle Michel.'

'You will be wicked in every way,' said the priest.

'No, M. le Curé. If I had married M. Urmand, I know I should be wicked to leave him, and I would do my best to live with him and make him a good wife. But I have found out in time that I can't love him; and therefore I am sure that I ought not to marry him, and I won't.'

There was much more said between them, but M. le Curé Gondin was not able to prevail in the least. He tried to cajole her, and he tried to persuade by threats, and he tried to conquer her by gratitude and affection towards her uncle. But he could not prevail at all.

'It is of no use my staying here any longer, M. le Curé,' she said at last, 'because I am quite sure that nothing on earth will induce me to consent. I am very sorry for what I have done. If you tell me that I have sinned, I will repent and confess it. I have repented, and am very, very sorry. I know now that I was very wrong ever to think it possible that I could be his wife. But you can't make me think that I am wrong in this.'

Then she left him, and as soon as she was gone, Madame Voss returned to hear the priest's report as to his success.

In the mean time, Michel Voss had reached Basle, arriving there some five hours before Marie's letter, and, in his ignorance of the law, had made his futile attempt to intercept the letter before it reached the hands of M. Urmand. But he was with Urmand when the letter was delivered, and endeavoured to persuade his young friend not to open it. But in doing this he was obliged to explain, to a certain extent, what was the nature of the letter. He was obliged to say so much about it as to justify the unhappy lover in asserting that it would be better for them all that he should know the contents. 'At any rate, you will promise not to believe it,' said Michel. And he did succeed in obtaining from M. Urmand a sort of promise that he would not regard the words of the letter as in truth expressing Marie's real resolution. 'Girls, you know, are such queer cattle,' said Michel. 'They think about all manner of things, and then they don't know what they are thinking.'

'But who is the other man?' demanded Adrian, as soon as he had finished the letter. Any one judging from his countenance when he asked the question would have imagined that in spite of his promise he believed every word that had been written to him. His face was a picture of blank despair, and his voice was low and hoarse. 'You must know whom she means,' he added, when Michel did not at once reply.

'Yes; I know whom she means.'

'Who is it then, M. Voss?'

'It is George, of course,' replied the innkeeper.

'I did not know,' said poor Adrian Urmand.

'She never spoke a dozen words to any other man in her life, and as for him, she has hardly seen him for the last eighteen months. He has come over and said something to her, like a traitor, - has reminded her of some childish promise, some old vow, something said when they were children, and meaning nothing; and so he has frightened her.'

'I was never told that there was anything between them,' said Urmand, beginning to think that it would become him to be indignant.

'There was nothing to tell, - literally nothing.'

'They must have been writing to each other.'

'Never a line; on my word as a man. It was just as I tell you. When George went from home, there had been some fooling, as I thought, between them; and I was glad that he should go. I didn't think it meant anything, or ever would.' As Michel Voss said this, there did occur to him an idea that perhaps, after all, he had been wrong to interfere in the first instance, - that there had then been no really valid reason why George should not have married Marie Bromar; but that did not in the least influence his judgment as to what it might be expedient to do now. He was still as sure as ever that as things stood now, it was his duty to do all in his power to bring about the marriage between his niece and Adrian Urmand. 'But since that, there has been nothing,' continued he, 'absolutely nothing. Ask her, and she will tell you so. It is some romantic idea of hers that she ought to stick to her first promise, now that she has been reminded of it.'

All this did not convince Adrian Urmand, who for a while expressed his opinion that it would be better for him to take Marie's refusal, and thus to let the matter drop. It would be very bitter to him, because all Basle had now heard of his proposed marriage, and a whole shower of congratulations had already fallen upon him from his fellow-townspeople: but he thought that it would be more bitter to be rejected again in person by Marie Bromar, and then to be stared at by all the natives of Granpere. He acknowledged that George Voss was a traitor; and would have been ready to own that Marie was another, had Michel Voss given him any encouragement in that direction. But Michel throughout the whole morning, - and they were closeted together for hours, - declared that poor Marie was more sinned against than sinning. If Adrian was but once more over at Granpere, all would be made right. At last Michel Voss prevailed, and persuaded the young man to return with him to the Lion d'Or.

They started early on the following morning, and travelled to Granpere by way of Colmar and the mountain. The father thus passed twice through Colmar, but on neither occasion did he call upon his son.

Chapter 17

There had been very little said between Michel Voss and Urmand on their journey towards Granpere till they were at the top of the Vosges, on the mountain road, at which place they had to leave their little carriage and bait their horse. Indeed Michel had been asleep during almost the entire time. On the night but one before he had not been in bed at all, having reached Basle after midnight, and having passed the hours 'twixt that and his morning visit to Urmand's house in his futile endeavours to stop poor Marie's letter. And the departure of the travellers from Basle on this morning had been very early, so that the poor innkeeper had been robbed of his proper allowance of natural rest. He had slept soundly in the train to Colmar, and had afterwards slept in the little *calèche* which had taken them to the top of the mountain. Urmand had sat silent by his side, - by no means anxious to disturb his companion, because he had no determined plan ready to communicate. Once or twice before he reached Colmar he had thought that he would go back again. He had been, he felt, badly treated; and, though he was very fond of Marie, it would be better for him perhaps to wash his hands of the whole affair. He was so thinking the whole way to Colmar. But he was afraid of Michel Voss, and when they got out upon the platform there, he had no resolution ready to be declared as fixed. Then they had hired the little carriage, and Michel Voss had slept again. He had slept all through Münster, and up the steep mountain, and was not thoroughly awake till they were summoned to get out at the wonderfully fine house for refreshment which the late Emperor caused to be built at the top of the hill. Here they went into the restaurant, and as Michel Voss was known to the man who kept it, he ordered a bottle of wine. 'What a terrible place to live in all the winter!' he said, as he looked down through the window right into the deep valley below. From the spot on which the house is built you can see all the broken wooded ground of the steep descent, and then the broad plain that stretches away to the valley of the Rhine. 'There is nothing but snow here after Christmas,' continued Michel, 'and perhaps not a Christian over the road for days together. I shouldn't like it, I know. It may be all very well just now.'

But Adrian Urmand was altogether inattentive either to the scenery now before him, or to the prospect of the mountain innkeeper's winter life. He knew that two hours and a half would take them down the mountain into Granpere, and that when there, it would be at once necessary that he should begin a task the idea of which was by no means pleasant to him. He was quite sure now that he wished he had remained at Basle, and that he had accepted Marie's letter as final. He told himself again and again that he could not make her marry him if she chose to change her mind. What was he to say, and what was he to do when he got to Granpere, a place which he almost wished that he had never seen in spite of those profitable linen-buyings? And now when Michel Voss began to talk to him about the scenery, and what this man up in the mountain did in the winter, - at this moment when his terrible trouble was so very near him, - he felt it to be an insult, or at least a cruelty. 'What can he do from December till April except smoke and drink?' asked Michel Voss.

'I don't care what he does,' said Urmand, turning away. 'I only know I wish I'd never come here.'

'Take a glass of wine, my friend,' said Michel. 'The mountain air has made you chill.' Urmand took the glass of wine, but it did not cheer him much. 'We shall have it all right before the day is over,' continued Michel.

'I don't think it will ever be all right,' said the other.

'And why not? The fact is, you don't understand young women; as how should you, seeing that you have not had to manage them? You do as I tell you, and just be round with her. You tell her that you don't desire any change yourself, and that after what has passed you can't allow her to think of such a thing. You speak as though you had a downright claim, as you have; and all will come right. It's not that she cares for him, you know. You must remember that. She has never even said a word of that kind. I haven't a doubt on my mind as to which she really likes best; but it's that stupid promise, and the way that George has had of making her believe that she is bound by the first word she ever spoke to a young man. It's only nonsense, and of course we must get over it.' Then they were summoned out, the horse having finished his meal, and were rattled down the hill into Granpere without many more words between them.

One other word was spoken, and that word was hardly pleasant in its tone. Urmand at least did not relish it. 'I shall go away at once if she doesn't treat me as she ought,' said he, just as they were entering the village.

Michel was silent for a moment before he answered. 'You'll behave, I'm sure, as a man ought to behave to a young woman whom he intends to make his wife.' The words themselves were civil enough; but there was a tone in the innkeeper's voice and a flame in his eye, which made Urmand almost feel that he had been threatened. Then they drove into the space in front of the door of the Lion d'Or.

Michel had made for himself no plan whatsoever. He led the way at once into the house, and Urmand followed, hardly daring to look up into the faces of the persons around him. They were both of them soon in the presence of Madame Voss, but Marie Bromar was not there. Marie had been sharp enough to perceive who was coming before they were out of the carriage, and was already ensconced in some safer retreat up-stairs, in which she could meditate on her plan of the campaign. 'Look lively, and get us something to eat,' said Michel, meaning to be cheerful and self-possessed. 'We left Basle at five, and have not eaten a mouthful since.' It was now nearly four o'clock, and the bread and cheese which had been served with the wine on the top of the mountain had of course gone for nothing. Madame Voss immediately began to bustle about, calling the cook and Peter Veque to her assistance. But nothing for a while was said about Marie. Urmand, trying to look as though he were self-possessed, stood with his back to the stove, and whistled. For a few minutes, during which the bustling about the table went on, Michel was wrapped in thought, and said nothing. At last he had made up his mind, and spoke: 'We might as well make a dash at it at once,' said he. 'Where is Marie?' No one answered him. 'Where is Marie Bromar?' he asked again, angrily. He knew that it behoved him now to take upon himself at once the real authority of a master of a house.

'She is up-stairs,' said Peter, who was straightening a table-cloth.

'Tell her to come down to me,' said her uncle. Peter departed immediately, and for a while there was silence in the little room. Adrian Urmand felt his heart to palpitate disagreeably. Indeed, the manner in which it would appear that the innkeeper proposed to manage the business was distressing enough to him. It seemed as though it were intended that he should discuss his little difficulties with Marie in the presence of the whole household. But he stood his ground, and sounded one more ineffectual little whistle. In a few minutes Peter returned, but said nothing. 'Where is Marie Bromar?' again demanded Michel in an angry voice.

'I told her to come down,' said Peter.

'Well?'

'I don't think she's coming,' said Peter.

'What did she say?'

'Not a word; she only bade me go down.' Then Michel walked into the kitchen as though he were about to fetch the recusant himself. But he stopped himself, and asked his wife to go up to Marie. Madame Voss did go up, and after her return there was some whispering between her and her husband. 'She is upset by the excitement of your return,' Michel said at last; 'and we must give her a little grace. Come, we will eat our dinner.'

In the mean time Marie was sitting on her bed up-stairs in a most unhappy plight. She really loved her uncle, and almost feared him. She did fear him with that sort of fear which is produced by reverence and habits of obedience, but which, when softened by affection, hardly makes itself known as fear, except on troublous occasions. And she was oppressed by the remembrance of all that was due from her to him and to her aunt, feeling, as it was natural that she should do, in compliance with the manners and habits of her people, that she owed a duty of obedience in this matter of marriage. Though she had been able to hold her own against the priest, and had been quite firm in opposition to her aunt, - who was in truth a woman much less strong by nature than herself, - she dreaded a farther dispute with her uncle. She could not bear to think that he should be enabled to accuse her with justice of ingratitude. It had been her great pleasure to be true to him, and he had answered her truth by a perfect confidence which had given a charm to her life. Now this would all be over, and she would be driven again to beg him to send her away, that she might become a household drudge elsewhere. And now that this very moment of her agony had come, and that this man to whom she had given a promise was there to claim her, how was she to go down and say what she had to say, before all the world? It was perfectly clear to her that in accordance with her reception of Urmand at the first moment of their meeting, so must be her continued conduct towards him, till he should leave her, or else take her away with him. She could not smile on him and shake hands with him, and cut his bread for him and pour out his wine, after such a letter as she had written to him, without signifying thereby that the letter was to go for nothing. Now, let what might happen, the letter was not to go for nothing. The letter was to remain a true fact, and a true letter. 'I can't go down, Aunt Josey; indeed I can't,' she said. 'I am not well, and I should drop. Pray tell Uncle Michel, with my best love and with my duty, that I can't go to him now.' And she sat still upon her bed, not weeping, but clasping her hands, and trying to see her way out of her misfortune.

The dinner was eaten in grim silence, and after the dinner Michel, still grimly silent, sat with his friend on the bench before the door and smoked a cigar. While he was smoking, Michel said never a word. But he was thinking of the difficulty he had to overcome; and he was thinking also, at odd moments, whether his own son George was not, after all, a better sort of lover for a young woman than this young man who was seated by his side. But it never occurred to him that he might find a solution of the difficulty by encouraging this second idea. Urmand, during this time, was telling himself that it behoved him to be a man, and that his sitting there in silence was hardly proof of his manliness. He knew that he was being ill-treated, and that he must do something to redress his own wrongs, if he only knew how to do it. He was quite determined that he would not be a coward; that he would stand up for his own rights. But if a young woman won't marry a man, a man can't make her do so, either by scolding her, or by fighting any of her friends. In this case the young lady's friends were all on his side. But the weight of that half hour of silence and of Michel's gloom was intolerable to him. At last he got up and declared he would go and see an old woman who would have linen to sell. 'As I am here, I might as well do a stroke of work,' he said, striving to be jocose.

'Do,' said Michel; 'and in the mean time I will see Marie Bromar.'

Whenever Michel Voss was heard to call his niece Marie Bromar, using the two names, it was understood, by all who heard him about the hotel, that he was not in a good humour. As soon as Urmand was gone, he rose slowly from his seat, and with heavy steps he went up-stairs in search of the refractory girl. He went straight to her own bedroom, and there he found her still sitting on her bedside. She jumped up as soon as he was in the room, and running up to him, took him by the arm. 'Uncle Michel,' she said, 'pray, pray be good to me. Pray, spare me!'

'I am good to you,' he said. 'I try to be good to you.'

'You know that I love you. Do you not know that I love you?' Then she paused, but he made no answer to her. He was surer of nothing in the world than he was of her affection; but it did not suit him to acknowledge it at that moment. 'I would do anything for you that I could do, Uncle Michel; but pray do not ask me to do this?' Then she clasped him tightly, and hung upon him, and put up her face to be kissed. But he would not kiss her. 'Ah,' said she; 'you mean to be hard to me. Then I must go; then I must go; then I must go.'

'That is nonsense, Marie. You cannot go, till you go to your husband. Where would you go to?'

'It matters not where I go to now.'

'Marie, you are betrothed to this man, and you must consent to become his wife. Say that you will consent, and all this nonsense shall be forgotten.' She did not say that she would consent; but she did not say that she would not, and he thought that he might persuade her, if he could speak to her as he ought. But he doubted which might be most efficacious, affection or severity. He had assured himself that it would be his duty to be very severe, before he gave up the point; but it might be possible, as she was so sweet with him, so loving and so gracious, that affection might prevail. If so, how much easier would the task be to himself! So he put his arm round her, and stooped down and kissed her.

'O, Uncle Michel,' she said; 'dear, dear Uncle Michel; say that you will spare me, and be on my side, and be good to me.'

'My darling girl, it is for your own good, for the good of us all, that you should marry this man. Do you not know that I would not tell you so, if it were not true? I cannot be more good to you than that.'

'I can - not, Uncle Michel.'

'Tell me why, now. What is it? Has anybody been bringing tales to you?'

'Nobody has brought any tales.'

'Is there anything amiss with him?'

'It is not that. It is not that at all. I am sure he is an excellent young man, and I wish with all my heart he had a better wife than I can ever be.'

'He thinks you will be quite good enough for him.'

'I am not good for anybody. I am very bad.'

'Leave him to judge of that.'

'But I cannot do it, Uncle Michel. I can never be Adrian Urmand's wife.'

'But why, why, why?' repeated Michel, who was beginning to be again angered by his own want of success. 'You have said that a dozen times, but have never attempted to give a reason.'

'I will tell you the reason. It is because I love George with all my heart, and with all my soul. He is so dear to me, that I should always be thinking of him. I could not help myself. I should always have him in my heart. Would that be right, Uncle Michel, if I were married to another man?'

'Then why did you accept the other man? There is nothing changed since then.'

'I was wicked then.'

'I don't think you were wicked at all; - but at any rate you did it. You didn't think anything about having George in your heart then.'

It was very hard for her to answer this, and for a moment or two she was silenced. At last she found a reply. 'I thought everything was dead within me then, - and that it didn't signify. Since that he has been here, and he has told me all.'

'I wish he had stayed where he was with all my heart. We did not want him here,' said the innkeeper in his anger.

'But he did come, Uncle Michel. I did not send for him, but he did come.'

'Yes; he came, - and he has disturbed everything that I had arranged so happily. Look here, Marie. I lay my commands upon you as your uncle and guardian, and I may say also as your best and stanchest friend, to be true to the solemn engagement which you have made with this young man. I will not hear any answer from you now, but I leave you with that command. Urmand has come here at my request, because I told him that you would be obedient. If you make a fool of me, and of yourself, and of us all, it will be impossible that I should forgive you. He will see you this evening, and I will trust to your good sense to receive him with propriety.' Then Michel Voss left the room and descended with ponderous steps, indicative of a heavy heart.

Marie, when she was alone, again seated herself on the bedside. Of course she must see Adrian Urmand. She was quite aware that she could not encounter him now with that half-saucy independent air which had come to her quite naturally before she had accepted him. She would willingly humble herself in the dust before him, if by so doing she could induce him to relinquish his suit. But if she could not do so; if she could not talk over either her uncle or him to be on what she called her side, then what should she do? Her uncle's entreaties to her, joined to his too evident sorrow, had upon her an effect so powerful, that she could hardly overcome it. She had, as she thought, resolved most positively that nothing should induce her to marry Adrian Urmand. She had of course been very firm in this resolution when she wrote her letter. But now - now she was almost shaken! When she thought only of herself, she would almost task herself to believe that after all it did not much matter what of happiness or of unhappiness might befall her. If she allowed herself to be taken to a new home at Basle she could still work and eat and drink, - and working, eating, and drinking she could wait till her unhappiness should be removed. She was sufficiently wise to understand that as she became a middle-aged woman, with perhaps children around her, her sorrow would melt into a soft regret which would be at

144

least endurable. And what did it signify after all how much one such a being as herself might suffer? The world would go on in the same way, and her small troubles would be of but little significance. Work would save her from utter despondence. But when she thought of George, and the words in which he had expressed the constancy of his own love, and the shipwreck which would fall upon him if she were untrue to him, - then again she would become strong in her determination. Her uncle had threatened her with his lasting displeasure. He had said that it would be impossible that he should forgive her. That would be unbearable! Yet, when she thought of George, she told herself that it must be borne.

Before the hour of supper came, her aunt had been with her, and she had promised to see her suitor alone. There had been some doubt on this point between Michel and his wife, Madame Voss thinking that either she or her husband ought to be present. But Michel had prevailed. 'I don't care what any people may say,' he replied. 'I know my own girl; - and I know also what he has a right to expect.' So it was settled, and Marie understood that Adrian was to come to her in the little brightly furnished sitting-room upstairs. On this occasion she took no notice of the hotel supper at all. It is to be hoped that Peter Veque proved himself equal to the occasion.

At about nine she was seated in the appointed place, and Madame Voss brought her lover up into the room.

'Here is M. Urmand come to speak to you,' she said. 'Your uncle thinks that you had better see him alone. I am sure you will bear in mind what it is that he and I wish.' Then she closed the door, and Adrian and Marie were left together.

'I need hardly tell you,' said he, 'what were my feelings when your uncle came to me yesterday morning. And when I opened your letter and read it, I could hardly believe that it had come from you.'

'Yes, M. Urmand; - it did come from me.'

'And why - what have I done? The last word you had spoken to me was to declare that you would be my loving wife.'

'Not that, M. Urmand; never that. When I thought it was to be so, I told you that I would do my best to do my duty by you.'

'Say that once more, and all shall be right.'

'But I never promised that I would love you. I could not promise that; and I was very wicked to allow them to give you my troth. You can't think worse of me than I think of myself.'

'But, Marie, why should you not love me? I am sure you would love me.'

'Listen to me, M. Urmand; listen to me, and be generous to me. I think you can be generous to a poor girl who is very unhappy. I do not love you. I do not say that I should not have loved you, if you had been the first. Why should not any girl love you? You are above me in every way, and rich, and well spoken of; and your life has been less rough and poor than mine. It is not that I have been proud. What is there that I can be proud of - except my uncle's trust in me? But George Voss had come to me before, and had made me promise that I would love him; - and I do love him. How can I help it, if I wished to help it? O, M. Urmand, can you not be generous? Think how little it is that you will lose.' But Adrian Urmand did not like to be told of the girl's love for another man. His generosity would almost have been more easily reached had she told him of George's love for her. People had assured him since he was engaged that Marie Bromar was the handsomest girl in Lorraine or Alsace; and he felt it to be an injury that this handsome girl should prefer such a one as George Voss to himself. Marie, with a woman's sharpness, perceived all this accurately. 'Remember,' said she, 'that I had hardly seen you when George and I were - when he and I became such friends.'

'Your uncle doesn't want you to marry his son.'

'I shall never become George's wife without consent; never.'

'Then what would be the use of my giving way?' asked Urmand. 'He would never consent.'

She paused for a moment before she replied.

'To save yourself,' said she, 'from living with a woman who cannot love you, and to save me from living with a man I cannot love.'

'And is this to be all the answer you will give me?'

'It is the request that I have to make to you,' said Marie.

'Then I had better go down to your uncle.' And he went down to Michel Voss, leaving Marie Bromar again alone.

Chapter 18

The people of Colmar think Colmar to be a considerable place, and far be it from us to hint that it is not so. It is - or was in the days when Alsace was French - the chief town of the department of the Haut Rhine. It bristles with barracks, and is busy with cotton factories. It has been accustomed to the presence of a préfet, and is no doubt important. But it is not so large that people going in and out of it can pass without attention, and this we take to be the really true line of demarcation between a big town and a little one. Had Michel Voss and Adrian Urmand passed through Lyons or Strasbourg on their journey to Granpere, no one would have noticed them, and their acquaintances in either of those cities would not have been a bit the wiser. But it was not probable that they should leave the train at the Colmar station, and hire Daniel Bredin's *calèche* for the mountain journey thence to Granpere, without all the facts of the case coming to the ears of Madame Faragon. And when she had heard the news, of course she told it to George Voss. She had interested herself very keenly in the affair of George's love, partly because she had a soft heart of her own and loved a ray of romance to fall in upon her as she sat fat and helpless in her easy-chair, and partly because she thought that the future landlord of the Hôtel de la Poste at Colmar ought to be regarded as a bigger man and a better match than any Swiss linen-merchant in the world. 'I can't think what it is that your father means,' she had said. 'When he and I were young, he used not to be so fond of the people of Basle, and he didn't think so much then of a peddling buyer of sheetings and shirtings.' Madame Faragon was rather fond of alluding to past times, and of hinting to George that in early days, had she been willing, she might have been mistress of the Lion d'Or at Granpere, instead of the Poste at Colmar. George never quite believed the boast, as he knew that Madame Faragon was at least ten years older than his father. 'He used to think,' continued Madame Faragon, 'that there was nothing better than a good house in the public line, with a well-spirited woman inside it to stand her ground and hold her own. But everything is changed now, since the railroads came up. The pedlars become merchants, and the respectable old shopkeepers must go to the wall.' George would hear all this in silence, though he knew that his old friend was endeavouring to comfort him by making little of the Basle linen-merchant. Now, when Madame Faragon learned that Michel Voss and Adrian Urmand had gone through Colmar back from Basle on their way to Granpere, she immediately foresaw what was to happen. Marie's marriage was to be hurried on, George was to be thrown overboard, and the pedlar's pack was to be triumphant over the sign of the innkeeper.

'If I were you, George, I would dash in among them at once,' said Madame Faragon.

George was silent for a minute or two, leaving the room and returning to it before he made any answer. Then he declared that he would dash in among them at Granpere.

'It will be better to go over and see it all settled,' he said.

'But, George, you won't quarrel?'

'What do you mean by quarrelling? I don't suppose that this man and I can be very dear friends when we meet each other.'

'You won't have any fighting? O, George, if I thought there was going to be fighting, I would go myself to prevent it.' Madame Faragon no doubt was sincere in her desire that there should be no fighting; but, nevertheless, there was a life and reality about this little affair which had a gratifying effect upon her. 'If I thought I could do any good, I really would go,' she said again afterwards. But George did not encourage her to make the attempt.

No more was said about it; but early on the following morning, or in truth long before the morning had dawned, George had started upon his journey, following his father and M. Urmand in their route over the mountain. This was the third time he had gone to Granpere in the course of the present autumn, and on each time he had gone without invitation and without warning. And yet, previous to this, he had remained above a year at Colmar without taking any notice of his family. He

148

knew that his father would not make him welcome, and he almost doubted whether it would be proper for him to drive himself direct to the door of the hotel. His father had told him, when they were last parting from each other, that he was nothing but a trouble. 'You are all trouble,' his father had said to him. And then his father had threatened to have him turned from the door by the servants, if he should come to the house again before Marie and Adrian were married. He was not afraid of his father; but he felt that he had no right to treat the Lion d'Or as his own home unless he was prepared to obey his father. And he knew nothing as to Marie and her purpose. He had learned from her that, were she left to herself, she would give herself with all her heart to him. But she would not be left to herself, and he only knew now that Adrian Urmand was being taken back to Granpere, - of course with the intention that the marriage should be at once perfected. Madame Faragon had, no doubt, been right in her advice as to dashing in among them at once. Whatever was to be done must be done now. But it was by no means clear to him how he was to carry on the war when he found himself among them all at Granpere.

It was now October, and the morning on the mountain was very dark and cold. He had started from Colmar between three and four, so that he had passed through Münster, and was ascending the hill before six. He stopped, too, and fed his horse at the Emperor's house at the top, and fortified himself with a tumbler of wine and a hunch of bread. He meant to go into Granpere and claim Marie as his own. He would go to the priest, and to the pastor if necessary, and forbid all authorities to lend their countenance to the proposed marriage. He would speak his mind plainly, and would accuse his father of extreme cruelty. He would call upon Madame Voss to save her niece. He would be very savage with Marie, hoping that he might thereby save her from herself, - defying her to say either before man or God that she loved the man whom she was about to make her husband. And as to Adrian Urmand himself - ; he still thought that, should the worst come to the worst, he would try some process of choking upon Adrian Urmand. Any use of personal violence would be distasteful to him and contrary to his nature. He was not a man who in the ordinary way of his life would probably lift his hand against another. Such liftings of hands on the part of other men he regarded as a falling back to the truculence of savage life. Men should manage and coerce each other either with the tongue, or with money, or with the law - according to his theory of life. But on such an occasion as this he found himself obliged to acknowledge that, if the worst should come to the worst, some attempt at choking his enemy must be made. It must be made for Marie's sake, if not for his own. In this mood of mind he drove down to Granpere, and, not knowing where else to stop, drew up his horse in the middle of the road before the hotel. The stable-servant, who was hanging about, immediately came to him; - and there was his father standing, all alone, at the door of the house. It was now ten o'clock, and he had expected that his father would have been away from home, as was his custom at that hour. But the innkeeper's mind was at present too full of trouble to allow of his going off either to the woodcutting or to the farm.

Adrian Urmand, after his failure with Marie on the preceding evening, had not again gone down-stairs. He had taken himself at once to his bedroom, and had remained there gloomy and unhappy, very angry with Marie Bromar; but, if possible, more angry with Michel Voss. Knowing, as he must have known, how the land lay, why had the innkeeper brought him from Basle to Granpere? He found himself to have been taken in, from first to last, by the whole household, and he would at this moment have been glad to obliterate Granpere altogether from among the valleys of the Vosges. And so he went to bed in his wrath. Michel and Madame Voss sat below waiting for him above an hour. Madame Voss more than once proposed that she should go up and see what was happening. It was impossible, she declared, that they should be talking together all that time. But her husband had stayed her. 'Whatever they have to say, let them say it out.' It seemed to him that Marie must be giving way, if she submitted herself to so long an interview. When at last Madame Voss did go up-stairs, she learned from the maid that M. Urmand had been in bed ever so long; and on going to Marie's chamber, she found her sitting where she had sat before. 'Yes, Aunt Josey, I will go to bed at once,' she said. 'Give uncle my love.' Then Aunt Josey had returned to her husband,

and neither of them had been able to extract any comfort from the affairs of the evening.

Early on the following morning, M. le Curé was called to a consultation. This was very distasteful to Michel Voss, because he was himself a Protestant, and, having lived all his life with a Protestant son and two Roman Catholic women in the house, he had come to feel that Father Gondin's religion was a religion for the weaker sex. He troubled himself very little with the doctrinal differences, having no slightest touch of an idea that he was to be saved because he was a Protestant, and that they were in peril because they were Roman Catholics. Nor, indeed, was there any such idea on either side prevalent in the valley. What M. le Curé himself may have believed, who can say? But he never taught his parishioners that their Protestant uncles and wives and children were to be damned. Michel Voss was averse to priestly assistance; but now he submitted to it. He hardly knew himself how far that betrothal was a binding ceremony. But he felt strongly that he had committed himself to the marriage; that it did not become him to allow that his son had been right; and also that if Marie would only marry the man, she would find herself quite happy in her new home. So M. le Curé was called in, and there was a consultation. M. le Curé was quite as hot in favour of the marriage as were the other persons concerned. It was, in the first place, infinitely preferable in his eyes that his young parishioner should marry a Roman Catholic. But he was not able to undertake to use any special thunders of the Church. He could tell the young woman what was her duty, and he had done so. If her guardians wished it, he would do so again, very strongly. But he did not know how he was to do more. Then the priest told the story of Annette Lolme, pointing out how well Marie was acquainted with all the bearings of the case.

'But both consented to break it off in that case,' said Michel. It was singular to observe how cruel he had become against the girl whom he so dearly loved. The Curé explained to him again that neither the Church nor the law could interfere to make her marry M. Urmand. It might be explained to her that she would commit a sin requiring penitence and absolution if she did not marry him. The Church could go no farther than that. But - such was the Curé's opinion - there was no power at the command of Michel Voss by which he could force his niece to marry the man, unless his own internal power as a friend and a protector might enable him to do so. 'She doesn't care a straw for that now,' said he. 'Not a straw. Since that fellow was over here, she thinks nothing of me, and nothing of her word.' Then he went out to the hotel door, leaving the priest with his wife, and he had not stood there for a minute or two before he saw his son's arrival. Marie, in the mean time, had not left her room. She had sent word down to her uncle that she was ill, and that she would beg him to go up to her. As yet he had not seen her; but a message had been taken to her, saying that he would come soon. Adrian Urmand had breakfasted alone, and had since been wandering about the house by himself. He also, from the windows of the billiard-room, had seen the arrival of George Voss.

Michel Voss, when he saw George, did not move from his place. He was still very angry with his son, vehemently angry, because his son stood in the way of the completion of his desires. But he had forgotten all his threats, spoken now nearly a week ago. He was altogether oblivious of his declaration that he would have George turned away from the door by the servants of the inn. That his own son should treat his house as a home was so natural to him, that it did not even occur to him now that he could bid him not to enter. There he was again, creating more trouble; and, as far as our friend the innkeeper could see, likely enough to be successful in his object. Michel stood his ground, with his hands in his pockets, because he would not even shake hands with his son. But when George came up, he bowed a recognition with his head; as though he should have said, 'I see you; but I cannot say that you are welcome to Granpere.' George stood for a moment or two, and then addressed his father.

'Adrian Urmand is here with you, is he not, father?'

'He is in the house somewhere,' said Michel, sullenly.

'May I speak to him?'

'I am not his keeper; not his,' and Michel put a special accent on the last word, by which he implied that though he was not the keeper of Adrian Urmand, he was the keeper of somebody else. George stood awhile, hesitating, by his father's side, and as he stood he saw through the window of the billiard-room the

152

figure of Urmand, who was watching them. 'Your mother is in her own room; you had better go to her,' said Michel. Then George entered the hotel, and his father went across the court to seek Urmand in his retreat. In this way the difficulty of the first meeting was overcome, and George did not find himself turned out of the Lion d'Or.

He knew of course nothing of the state of affairs at the inn. It might be that Marie had already given way, and was still the promised bride of this man. Indeed, to him it seemed most probable that such should be the case. He had been sent to look for Madame Voss, and Madame Voss he found in the kitchen.

'O, George, who expected to see you here to-day!' she exclaimed.

'Nobody, I daresay,' he replied. The cook was there, and two or three other servants and hangers-on. It was impossible that he should speak out before so many persons, and he had not a friend about the place, unless Marie was his friend. After a few moments he went into the inner room, and Madame Voss followed him. 'Well,' said he, 'has anything been settled?'

'I am sorry to say that everything is as unsettled as it can be,' said Madame Voss.

Then Marie must be true to him! And if so, she must be the grandest woman, the finest girl that had ever been created. If so, would he not be true to her? If so, with what a true worship would he offer her all that he had to give in the world! He had come there before determined to crush her with his thunderbolt. Now he would swear to cherish her and keep her warm with his love for ever and ever. 'Is she here?' he asked.

'She is up-stairs, in bed. You cannot see her.'

'She is not ill?'

'She is making everybody else ill about the place, I know that,' said Madame Voss. 'And as for you, George, you owe a different kind of treatment to your father; you do indeed. It will make an old man of him. He has set his heart upon this, and you ought to have yielded.'

It was at any rate evident that Marie was holding out, was true to her first love, in spite of that betrothal which had appeared to George to be so wicked, but which had in truth been caused by his own fault. If Marie would hold out, there would be no need that he should lay violent hands upon Adrian Urmand, or have resort to any process of choking. If she would only be firm, they could not succeed in making her marry the linen-merchant. He was not in the least afraid of M. le Curé Gondin; nor was he afraid of Adrian Urmand. He was not much afraid of Madame Voss. He was afraid only of his father. 'A man cannot yield on such a matter,' he said. 'No man yields in such an affair, - though he may be beaten.' Madame Voss listened to him, but said nothing farther. She was busy with her work, and went on intently with her needle.

He had asked to see Urmand, and he now went out in quest of him. He passed across the court, and in at the door of the café, and up into the billiard-room. Here he found both his father and the young man. Urmand got up to salute him, and George took off his hat. Nothing could be more ceremonious than the manner in which the two rivals greeted each other. They had not seen each other for nearly two years, and had never been intimate. When George had been living at Granpere, Urmand had only been an occasional sojourner at the inn, and had not as yet fallen into habits of friendship with the Voss family.

'Have you seen your mother?' Michel asked.

'Yes; I have seen her.' Then there was silence for awhile. Urmand knew not how to speak, and George was doubtful how to proceed in presence of his father.

Then Michel asked another question. 'Are you going to stay long with us, George?'

'Certainly not long, father. I have brought nothing with me but what you see.'

'You have brought too much, if you have come to give us trouble.'

Then there was another pause, during which George sat down in a corner, apart from them. Urmand took out a cigar and lit it, offering one to the innkeeper. But Michel Voss shook his head. He was very unhappy, feeling that everything around him was wrong. Here was a son of his, of whom he was proud, the only living child of his first wife, a young man of whom all people said good things; a son whom he had always loved and trusted, and who even now, at this very moment, was showing himself to be a real man; and yet he was forced to quarrel with this son, and say harsh things to him, and sit away from him with a man who was after all no more than a stranger to him, with whom he had no sympathy; when it would have made him so happy to be leaning on his son's shoulder, and discussing their joint affairs with unreserved confidence, asking questions about wages, and suggesting possible profits. He was beginning to hate Adrian Urmand. He was beginning to hate the young man, although he knew that it was his duty to go on with the marriage. Urmand, as soon as his cigar was lighted, got up and began to knock the balls about on the table. That gloom of silence was to him most painful.

'If you would not mind it, M. Urmand,' said George, 'I should like to take a walk with you.'

'To take a walk?'

'If it would not be disagreeable. Perhaps it would be well that you and I should have a few minutes of conversation.'

'I will leave you together here,' said the father, 'if you, George, will promise me that there shall be no violence.' Urmand looked at the innkeeper as though he did not like the proposition, but Michel took no notice of his look.

'There certainly shall be none on my part,' said George. 'I don't know what M. Urmand's feelings may be.'

'O dear, no; nothing of the kind,' said Urmand. 'But I don't exactly see what we are to talk about.' Michel, however, paid no attention to this, but walked slowly out of the room. 'I really don't know what there is to say,' continued Urmand, as he knocked the balls about with his cue.

'There is this to say. That girl up there was induced to promise that she would be your wife, when she believed that - I had forgotten her.'

'O dear, no; nothing of the kind.'

'That is her story. Go and ask her. If it is so, or even if it suits her now to say so, you will hardly, as a man, endeavour to drive her into a marriage which she does not wish. You will never do it, even if you do try. Though you go on trying till you drive her mad, she will never be your wife. But if you are a man, you will not continue to torment her, simply because you have got her uncle to back you.'

'Who says she will never marry me?'

'I say so. She says so.'

'We are betrothed to each other. Why should she not marry me?'

'Simply because she does not wish it. She does not love you. Is not that enough? She does love another man; me - me - me. Is not that enough? Heaven and earth! I would sooner go to the galleys, or break stones upon the roads, than take a woman to my bosom who was thinking of some other man.'

'That is all very fine.'

'Let me tell you, that the other thing, that which you propose to do, is by no means fine. But I will not quarrel with you, if I can help it. Will you go away and leave us at peace? They say you are rich and have a grand house. Surely you can do better than marry a poor innkeeper's niece - a girl that has worked hard all her life?'

'I could do better if I chose,' said Adrian Urmand.

'Then go and do better. Do you not perceive that even my father is becoming tired of all the trouble you are making? Surely you will not wait till you are turned out of the house?'

'Who will turn me out of the house?'

'Marie will, and my father. Do you think he'll see her wither and droop and die, or perhaps go mad, in order that a promise may be kept to you? Take the matter into your own hands at once, and say you will have no more to do with it. That will be the manly way.'

'Is that all you have to say, my friend?' asked Urmand, assuming a voice that was intended to be indifferent.

'Yes - that is all. But I mean to do something more, if I am driven to it.'

'Very well. When I want advice from you, I will come to you for it. And as for your doing, I believe you are not master here as yet. Good-morning.' So saying, Adrian Urmand left the room, and George Voss in a few minutes followed him down the stairs.

The rest of the day was passed in gloom and wretchedness. George hardly spoke to his father; but the two sat at table together, and there was no open quarrel between them. Urmand also sat with them, and tried to converse with Michel and Madame Voss. But Michel would say very little to him; and the mistress of the house was so cowed by the circumstances of the day, that she was hardly able to talk. Marie still kept her room; and it was stated to them that she was not well and was in bed. Her uncle had gone to see her twice, but had made no report to any one of what had passed between them.

It had come to be understood that George would sleep there, at any rate for that night, and a bed had been prepared for him. The party broke up very early, for there was nothing in common among them to keep them together. Madame Voss sat murmuring with the priest for half an hour or so; but it seemed that the gloom attendant upon the young lovers had settled also upon M. le Curé. Even he escaped as early as he could.

When George was about to undress himself there came a knock at his door, and one of the servant-girls put into his hand a scrap of paper. On it was written, 'I will never marry him, never - never - never; upon my honour!'

Chapter 19

Michel Voss at this time was a very unhappy man. He had taught himself to believe that it would be a good thing that his niece should marry Adrian Urmand, and that it was his duty to achieve this good thing in her behalf. He had had it on his mind for the last year, and had nearly brought it to pass. There was, moreover, now, at this present moment, a clear duty on him to be true to the young man who with his consent, and indeed very much at his instance, had become betrothed to Marie Bromar. The reader will understand how ideas of duty, not very clearly looked into or analysed, acted upon his mind. And then there was always present to him a recurrence of that early caution which had made him lay a parental embargo upon anything like love between his son and his wife's niece. Without much thinking about it, - for he probably never thought very much about anything, - he had deemed it prudent to separate two young people brought up together, when they began, as he fancied, to be foolish. An elderly man is so apt to look upon his own son as a boy, and on a girl who has grown up under his nose as little more than a child! And then George in those days had had no business of his own, and should not have thought of such a thing! In this way the mind of Michel Voss had been forced into strong hostility against the idea of a marriage between Marie and his son, and had filled itself with the spirit of a partisan on the side of Adrian Urmand. But now, as things had gone, he had been made very unhappy by the state of his own mind, and consequently was beginning to feel a great dislike for the merchant from Basle. The stupid mean little fellow, with his white pocket-handkerchief, and his scent, and his black greasy hair, had made his way into the house and had destroyed all comfort and pleasure! That was the light in which Michel was now disposed to regard his previously honoured guest. When he made a comparison between Adrian and

158

George, he could not but acknowledge that any girl of spirit and sense would prefer his son. He was very proud of his son, - proud even of the lad's disobedience to himself on such a subject; and this feeling added to his discomfort.

He had twice seen Marie in her bed during that day spoken of in the last chapter. On both occasions he had meant to be very firm; but it was not easy for such a one as Michel Voss to be firm to a young woman in her night-cap, rather pale, whose eyes were red with weeping. A woman in bed was to him always an object of tenderness, and a woman in tears, as his wife well knew, could on most occasions get the better of him. When he first saw Marie, he merely told her to lie still and take a little broth. He kissed her however and patted her cheek, and then got out of the room as quickly as he could. He knew his own weakness, and was afraid to trust himself to her prayers while she lay before him in that guise. When he went again, he had been unable not to listen to a word or two which she had prepared, and had ready for instant speech. 'Uncle Michel,' she said, 'I will never marry any one without your leave, if you will let M. Urmand go away.' He had almost come to wish by this time that M. Urmand would go away and never come back again. 'How am I to send him away?' he had said crossly. 'If you tell him, I know he will go, - at once,' said Marie. Michel had muttered something about Marie's illness and the impossibility of doing anything at present, and again had left the room. Then Marie began to take heart of grace, and to think that victory might yet be on her side. But how was George to know that she was firmly determined to throw those odious betrothals to the wind? Feeling it to be absolutely incumbent on her to convey to him this knowledge, she wrote the few words which the servant conveyed to her lover, - making no promise in regard to him, but simply assuring him that she would never, - never, - never become the wife of that other man.

Early on the following morning Michel Voss went off by himself. He could not stay in bed, and he could not hang about the house. He did not know how to demean himself to either of the young men when he met them. He could not be cordial as he ought to be with Urmand; nor could he be austere to George with that austerity which he felt would have been proper on his part. He was becoming very tired of his dignity and authority.

Hitherto the exercise of power in his household had generally been easy enough, his wife and Marie had always been loving and pleasant in their obedience. Till within these last weeks there had even been the most perfect accordance between him and his niece. 'Send him away; - that's very easily said,' he muttered to himself as he went up towards the mountains; 'but he has got my engagement, and of course he'll hold me to it.' He trudged on, he hardly knew whither. He was so unhappy, that the mills and the timber-cutting were nothing to him. When he had walked himself into a heat, he sat down and took out his pipe, but he smoked more by habit than for enjoyment. Supposing that he did bring himself to change his mind, - which he did not think he ever would, - how could he break the matter to Urmand? He told himself that he was sure he would not change his mind, because of his solemn engagement to the young man; but he did acknowledge that the young man was not what he had taken him to be. He was effeminate, and wanted spirit, and smelt of hair-grease. Michel had discovered none of these defects, - had perhaps regarded the characteristics as meritorious rather than otherwise, - while he had been hotly in favour of the marriage. Then the hair-grease and the rest of it had in his eyes simply been signs of the civilisation of the town as contrasted with the rusticity of the country. It was then a great thing in his eyes that Marie should marry a man so polished, though much of the polish may have come from pomade. Now his ideas were altered, and, as he sat alone upon the log, he continued to turn up his nose at poor M. Urmand. But how was he to be rid of him, - and, if not of him, what was he to do then? Was he to let all authority go by the board, and allow the two young people to marry, although the whole village heard how he had pledged himself in this matter?

As he was sitting there, suddenly his son came upon him. He frowned and went on smoking, though at heart he felt grateful to George for having found him out and followed him. He was altogether tired of being alone, or, worse than that, of being left together with Adrian Urmand. But the overtures for a general reconciliation could not come first from him, nor could any be entertained without at least some show of obedience. 'I thought I should find you up here,' said George.

'And now you have found me, what of that?'

'I fancy we can talk better, father, up among the woods, than we can down there when that young man is hanging about. We always used to have a chat up here, you know.'

'It was different then,' said Michel. 'That was before you had learned to think it a fine thing to be your own master and to oppose me in everything.'

'I have never opposed you but in one thing, father.'

'Ah, yes; in one thing. But that one thing is everything. Here I've been doing the best I could for both of you, striving to put you upon your legs, and make you a man and her a woman, and this is the return I get!'

'But what would you have had me do?'

'What would I have had you do? Not come here and oppose me in everything.'

'But when this Adrian Urmand - '

'I am sick of Adrian Urmand,' said Michel Voss. George raised his eyebrows and stared. 'I don't mean that,' said he; 'but I am beginning to hate the very sight of the man. If he'd had the pluck of a wren, he would have carried her off long ago.'

'I don't know how that may be, but he hasn't done it yet. Come, father; you don't like the man any more than she does. If you get tired of him in three days, what would she do in her whole life?'

'Why did she accept him, then?'

'Perhaps, father, we were all to blame a little in that.'

'I was not to blame - not in the least. I won't admit it. I did the best I could for her. She accepted him, and they are betrothed. The Curé down there says it's nearly as good as being married.'

'Who cares what Father Gondin says?' asked George.

'I'm sure I don't,' said Michel Voss.

'The betrothal means nothing, father, if either of them choose to change their minds. There was that girl over at Saint Die.'

'Don't tell me of the girl at Saint Die. I'm sick of hearing of the girl at Saint Die. What the mischief is the girl at Saint Die to us? We've got to do our duty if we can, like honest men and women; and not follow vagaries learned from Saint Die.'

The two men walked down the hill together, reaching the hotel about noon. Long before that time the innkeeper had fallen into a way of acknowledging that Adrian Urmand was an incubus; but he had not as yet quite admitted that there was any way of getting rid of the incubus. The idea of having the marriage on the 1st of the present month was altogether abandoned, and Michel had already asked how they might manage among them to send Adrian Urmand back to Basle. 'He must come again, if he chooses,' he had said; 'but I suppose he had better go now. Marie is ill, and she mustn't be worried.' George proposed that his father should tell this to Urmand himself; but it seemed that Michel, who had never yet been known to be afraid of any man, was in some degree afraid of the little Swiss merchant.

'Suppose my mother says a word to him,' suggested George.

'She wouldn't dare for her life,' answered the father.

'I would do it.'

'No, indeed, George; you shall do no such thing.'

Then George suggested the priest; but nothing had been settled when they reached the inn-door. There he was, swinging a cane at the foot of the billiard-room stairs - the little bug-a-boo, who was now so much in the way of all of them! The innkeeper muttered some salutation, and George just touched his hat. Then they both passed on, and went into the house.

Unfortunately the plea of Marie's illness was in part cut from under their feet by the appearance of Marie herself. George, who had not as yet seen her, went up quickly to her, and, without saying a word, took her by the hand and held it. Marie murmured some pretence at a salutation, but what she said was heard by no one. When her uncle came to her and kissed her, her hand was still grasped in that of George. All this had taken place in the passage; and before Michel's embrace was over, Adrian Urmand was standing in the doorway looking on. George, when he saw him, held tighter by the hand, and Marie made no attempt to draw it away.

'What is the meaning of all this?' said Urmand, coming up.

'Meaning of what?' asked Michel.

'I don't understand it - I don't understand it at all,' said Urmand.

'Don't understand what?' said Michel. The two lovers were still holding each other's hands; but Michel had not seen it; or, seeing it, had not observed it.

'Am I to understand that Marie Bromar is betrothed to me, or not?' demanded Adrian. 'When I get an answer either way, I shall know what to do.' There was in this an assumption of more spirit than had been expected on his part by his enemies at the Lion d'Or.

'Why shouldn't you be betrothed to her?' said Michel. 'Of course you are betrothed to her; but I don't see what is the use of your talking so much about it.'

'It is the first time I have said a word on the subject since I've been here,' said Urmand. Which was true; but as Michel was continually thinking of the betrothal, he imagined that everybody was always talking to him of the matter. Marie had now managed to get her hand free, and had retired into the kitchen. Michel followed her, and stood meditative, with his back to the large stove. As it happened, there was no one else present there at the moment.

'Tell him to go back to Basle,' whispered Marie to her uncle. Michel only shook his head and groaned.

'I don't think I am at all well-treated here among you,' said Adrian Urmand to George as soon as they were alone.

'Any special friendship from me you can hardly expect,' said George. 'As to my father and the rest of them, if they ill-treat you, I suppose you had better leave them.'

'I won't put up with ill-treatment from anybody. It's not what I'm used to.'

'Look here, M. Urmand,' said George. 'I quite admit you have been badly used; and, on the part of the family, I am ready to apologise.'

'I don't want any apology.'

'What do you want, M. Urmand?'

'I want - I want - Never mind what I want. It is from your father that I shall demand it, not from you. I shall take care to see myself righted. I know the French law as well as the Swiss.'

'If you're talking of law, you had better go back to Basle and get a lawyer,' said George.

163

There had been no word spoken of George returning to Colmar on that morning. He had told his father that he had brought nothing with him but what he had on; and in truth when he left Colmar he had not looked forward to any welcome which would induce him to remain at Granpere. But the course of things had been different from that which he had expected. He was much too good a general to think of returning now, and he had friends in the house who knew how to supply him with what was most necessary to him. Nobody had asked him to stay. His father had not uttered a word of welcome. But he did stay, and Michel would have been very much surprised indeed if he had heard that he had gone. The man in the stable had ventured to suggest that the old mare would not be wanted to go over the mountain that day. To this George assented, and made special request that the old mare might receive gentle treatment.

And so the day passed away. Marie, who had recovered her health, was busy as usual about the house. George and Urmand, though they did not associate, were rarely long out of each other's sight; and neither the one nor the other found much opportunity for pressing his suit. George probably felt that there was not much need to do so, and Urmand must have known that any pressing of his suit in the ordinary way would be of no avail. The innkeeper tried to make work for himself about the place, had the carriages out and washed, inspected the horses, and gave orders as to the future slaughter of certain pigs. Everybody about the house, nevertheless, down to the smallest boy attached to the inn, knew that the landlord's mind was pre-occupied with the love affairs of those two men. There was hardly an inhabitant of Granpere who did not understand what was going on; and, had it been the custom of the place to make bets on such matters, very long odds would have been wanted before any one would have backed Adrian Urmand. And yet two days ago he was considered to be sure of the prize. M. le Curé Gondin was a good deal at the hotel during the day, and perhaps he was the stanchest supporter of the Swiss aspirant. He endeavoured to support Madame Voss, having that strong dislike to yield an inch in practice or in doctrine, which is indicative of his order. He strove hard to make Madame Voss understand that if only she would be firm and cause her husband to be firm also, Marie would, of course, yield at last. 'I have ever so many young women just in the same way,' said the Curé, 'and you would have thought they were going to break their hearts; but as soon as ever they have been married, they have forgotten all that.' Madame Voss would have been quite contented to comply with the priest's counsel, could she have seen the way with her husband. But it had become almost manifest even to her, with the Curé to support her, that the star of Adrian Urmand was on the wane. She felt from every word that Marie spoke to her, that Marie herself was confident of success. And it may be said of Madame Voss, that although she had been forced by Michel into a kind of enthusiasm on behalf of the Swiss marriage, she had no very eager wishes of her own on the subject. Marie was her own niece, and was dear to her; but the girl was sure of a well-to-do husband whichever way the war went; and what aunt need desire more for her most favourite niece than a well-to-do husband?

The day went by, and the supper was eaten, and the cigars were smoked, and then they all went to bed. But nothing more had been settled. That obstinate young man, M. Adrian Urmand, though he had talked of his lawyer, had said not a word of going back to Basle.

Chapter 20

It is probable that all those concerned in the matter who slept at the Lion d'Or that night, made up their minds that on the following day the powers of the establishment must come to some decision. It was not right that a young woman should have to live in the house with two favoured lovers; nor, as regarded the young men, was it right that they should be allowed to go on glaring at each other. Both Michel and Madame Voss feared that they would do more than glare, seeing that they were so like two dogs with one bone between them, who, in such an emergency, will generally fight. Urmand himself was quite alive to the necessity of putting an end to his present exceptionally disagreeable position. He was very angry; very angry naturally with Marie, who had, he thought, treated him villainously. Why had she made that little soft, languid promise to him when he was last at Granpere, if she had not then loved him? And of course he was angry with George Voss. What unsuccessful lover fails of being angry with his happy rival? And then George had behaved with outrageous impropriety. Urmand was beginning now to have a clear insight of the circumstances. George and Marie had been lovers, and then George, having been sent away, had forgotten his love for a year or more. But when the girl had been accommodated with another lover, then he thrust himself forward and disturbed everybody's arrangements! No conduct could have been worse than this. But, nevertheless, Urmand's anger was the hottest against Michel Voss himself. Had he been left alone at Basle, had he been allowed to receive Marie's letter, and act upon it in accordance with his own judgment, he would never have made himself ridiculous by appearing at Granpere as a discomfited lover. But the innkeeper had come and dragged him away from home, had misrepresented everything, had carried him away, as it were, by force to the scene of his disgrace, and now

- threw him over! He, at any rate, he, Michel Voss, should, as Adrian Urmand felt very bitterly, have been true and constant; but Michel, whose face could not lie, whatever his words might do, was clearly as anxious to be rid of his young friend as were any of the others in the hotel. Urmand himself would have been very glad to be back at Basle. He had come to regard any farther connection with the inn at Granpere as extremely undesirable. The Voss family was low. He had found that out during his present visit. But how was he to get away, and not look, as he was going, like a dog with his tail between his legs? He had so clear a right to demand Marie's hand, that he could not bring himself to bear to be robbed of his claim. And yet he had come to perceive how very foolish such a marriage would be. He had been told that he could do better. Of course he could do better. But how could he be rid of his bargain without submitting to ill-treatment? If Michel had not come and fetched him away from his home the ill-treatment would have been by comparison slight, and of that normal kind to which young men are accustomed. But to be brought over to the house, and then to be deserted by everybody in the house! How, O how, was he to get out of the house? Such were his reflections as he sat solitary in the long public room drinking his coffee, and eating an omelet, with which Peter Veque had supplied him, but which had in truth been cooked for him very carefully by Marie Bromar herself. In her present frame of mind Marie would have cooked ortolans for him had he wished for them.

And while Urmand was eating his omelet and thinking of his wrongs, Michel Voss and his son were standing together at the stable door. Michel had been there some time before his son had joined him, and when George came up to him he put out his hand almost furtively. George grasped it instantly, and then there came a tear into the innkeeper's eye. 'I have brought you a little of that tobacco we were talking of,' said George, taking a small packet out of his pocket.

'Thank ye, George; thank ye; but it does not much matter now what I smoke. Things are going wrong, and I don't get satisfaction out of anything.'

'Don't say that, father.'

'How can I help saying it? Look at that fellow up there. What am I to do with him? What am I to say to him? He means to stay there till he gets his wife.'

'He'll never get a wife here, if he stays till the house falls on him.'

'I can see that now. But what am I to say to him? How am I to get rid of him? There is no denying, you know, that he has been treated badly among us.'

'Would he take a little money, father?'

'No. He's not so bad as that.'

'I should not have thought so; only he talked to me about his lawyer.'

'Ah; - he did that in his anger. By George, if I was in his position I should try and raise the very devil. But don't talk of giving him money, George. He's not bad in that way.'

'He shouldn't have said anything about his lawyer.'

'You wait till you're placed as he is, and you'll find that you'll say anything that comes uppermost. But what are we to do with him, George?'

Then the matter was discussed in the utmost confidence, and in all its bearings. George offered to have a carriage and pair of horses got ready for Remiremont, and then to tell the young man that he was expected to get into it, and go away; but Michel felt that there must be some more ceremonious treatment than that. George then suggested that the Curé should give the message, but Michel again objected. The message, he felt, must be given by himself. The doing this would be very bitter to him, because it would be necessary that he should humble himself before the scented shiny head of the little man: but Michel knew that it must be so. Urmand had been undoubtedly ill-treated among them, and the apology for that ill-treatment must be made by the chief of the family himself. 'I suppose I might as well go to him alone,' said Michel, groaning.

'Well, yes; I should say so,' replied his son. 'Soonest begun, soonest over; - and I suppose I might as well order the horses.'

To this latter suggestion the father made no reply, but went slowly into the house. He turned for a moment into Marie's little office, and stood there hesitating whether he would tell her his mission. As she was to be made happy, why should she not know it?

'You two have got the better of me among you,' he said.

'Which two, Uncle Michel?'

'Which two? Why, you and George. And what I'm to do with the gentleman upstairs, it passes me to think. Thank heaven, it will be a great many years before Flos wants a husband.' Flos was the little daughter up-stairs, who was as yet no more than five years old.

'I hope, Uncle Michel, you'll never have anybody else as naughty and troublesome as I have been,' said Marie, pressing close to him. She was indescribably happy. She was to be saved from the lover whom she did not want. She was to have the lover whom she did want. And, over and above all this, a spirit of kind feeling and full sympathy existed once more between her and her dear friend. As she offered no advice in regard to the disposal of the gentleman up-stairs, Michel was obliged to go upon his painful duty, trusting to his own wit.

In the long room up-stairs he found Adrian Urmand sitting at the closed window, looking out at the ducks who were paddling in a temporary pool made by the late rains. He had been painfully in want of something to do, - so much so that he had more than once almost resolved to put his things into his bag, and leave the house without saying a word of farewell to any one. Had there been any means for him to escape from Granpere without saying a word, he would have done so. But at Granpere there was no railway, and the only public conveyance in and out of the place started from the door of the Lion d'Or; started every morning, with much ceremony, so that it was impossible for him to fly unobserved. There he was, watching the ducks, when Michel entered the room, and very much disposed to quarrel with any one who approached him.

'I'm afraid you find it rather dull here,' said Michel, beginning the conversation.

'It is dull; very dull indeed.'

'That is the worst of it. We are dull people here in the country. We have not the distractions which you town folk can always find. There's not much to do, and nothing to look at.'

'Very little to look at, that's worth the trouble of looking,' said Urmand.

There was a malignity of satire intended in this; for the young man in his wrath, and with a full conviction of what was coming upon him, had intended to include his betrothed in the catalogue of things of Granpere not worthy of inspection. But Michel Voss did not at all follow him so far as that.

'I never saw such a place,' continued Urmand. 'There isn't a soul even to play a game of billiards with.'

Now Michel Voss, although for a purpose he had been willing to make little of his own village, did in truth consider that Granpere was at any rate as good a place to live in as Basle. And he felt that though he might abuse Granpere, it was very uncourteous in Adrian Urmand to do so. 'I don't think much of playing billiards in the morning, I must own,' said he.

'I daresay not,' said Urmand, still looking at the ducks.

Michel had made no progress as yet, so he sat down and scratched his head. The more he thought of it, the larger the difficulty seemed to be. He was quite aware now that it was his own unfortunate journey to Basle which had brought so heavy a burden on him. It was as yet no more than three or four days since he had taken upon himself to assure the young man that he, by his own authority, would make everything right; and now he was forced to acknowledge that everything was wrong.

'M. Urmand,' he said at last, 'it has been a very great grief to me, a very great grief indeed, that you should have found things so uncomfortable.'

'What things do you mean?' said Urmand.

'Well - everything - about Marie, you know. When I went over to Basle the other day, I didn't think how it was going to turn out. I didn't indeed.'

'And how is it going to turn out?'

'I can't make the young woman consent, you know,' said the innkeeper.

'Let me tell you, M. Voss, that I wouldn't have the young woman, as you call her, if she consented ever so much. She has disgraced me.'

To this Michel listened with perfect equanimity.

'She has disgraced you.'

At hearing this Michel bit his lips, telling himself, however, that there had been mistakes made, and that he was bound to bear a good deal.

'And she has disgraced herself,' said Adrian Urmand, with all the emphasis that he had at command.

'I deny it,' said Marie's uncle, coming close up to his opponent, and standing before him. 'I deny it. It is not true. That shall not be said in my hearing, even by you.'

'But I do say it. She has disgraced herself. Did she not give me her troth, when all the time she intended to marry another man?'

'No! She did nothing of the kind. And look here, my friend, if you wish to be treated like a man in this house, you had better not say anything against any of the women who live in it. You may abuse me as much as you please, - and George too, if it will do you any good. There have been mistakes made, and we owe you something.'

'By heavens, yes; you do.'

'But you sha'n't take it out in saying anything against Marie Bromar, - not in my hearing.'

'Why; - what will you do?'

'Don't drive me to do anything, M. Urmand. If there is any compensation possible - '

'Of course there must be compensation.'

'What is it you will take? Is it money?'

'Money; - no. As for money, I'm better off than any of you.'

'What is it, then? You don't want the girl herself?'

'No; - certainly not. I would not take her if she came and knelt to me.'

'What can we do, then? If you will only say.'

'I want - I want - I don't know what I want. I have been cruelly ill-used, and made a fool of before everybody. I never heard of such a case before; - never. And I have been so generous and honest to you! I did not ask for a franc of *dot*; and now you come and offer me money. I don't think any man ever was so badly used anywhere.' And on saying this Adrian Urmand in very truth burst into tears.

The innkeeper's heart was melted at once. It was all so true! Between them they had treated him very badly. But then there had been so many unfortunate and unavoidable mistakes! When the young man talked of compensation, what was Michel Voss to think? His son had been led into exactly the same error. Nevertheless, he repented himself bitterly in that he had

171

said anything about money, and was prepared to make the most abject apologies. Adrian Urmand had fallen into a chair, and Michel Voss came and seated himself close beside him.

'I beg your pardon, Urmand; I do indeed. I ought not to have mentioned money. But when you spoke of compensation - '

'It wasn't that. It wasn't that. It's my feelings!'

Then the white cambric handkerchief was taken out and used with considerable vehemence.

From that moment the innkeeper's goodwill towards Urmand returned, though of course he was quite aware that there was no place for him in that family.

'If there is anything I can do, I will do it,' said Michel piteously. 'It has been unfortunate. I know it has been very unfortunate. But we didn't mean to be untrue.'

'If you had only left me alone when I was at home?' said the unfortunate young man, who was still sobbing bitterly.

They two remained in the long room together for a considerable time, during all of which Michel Voss was as gentle as though Urmand had been a child. Nor did the poor rejected lover again have recourse to any violence of abuse, though he would over and over again repeat his opinion that surely, since lovers were first known in the world, and betrothals of marriage first made, no one had ever been so ill-used as was he. It soon became clear to Michel that his great grief did not come from the loss of his wife, but from the feeling that everybody would know that he had been ill-used. There wasn't a shopkeeper in his own town, he said, who hadn't heard of his approaching marriage. And what was he to say when he went back?

'Just say that you found us so rough and rustic,' said Michel Voss.

But Urmand knew well that no such saying on his part would be believed.

'I think I shall go to Lyons,' said he, 'and stay there for six months. What's the business to me? I don't care for the business.'

There they sat all the morning. Two or three times Peter Veque opened the door, peeped in at them, and then brought down word that the conference was still going on.

'The master is sitting just over him like,' said Peter, 'and they're as close and loving as birds.'

Marie listened, and said not a word to any one. George had made two or three little attempts during the morning to entice her into some lover-like privacy. But Marie would not be enticed. The man to whom she was betrothed was still in the house; and, though she was quite secure that the betrothals would now be absolutely annulled, still she would not actually entertain another lover till this was done.

At length the door of the long room was opened, and the two men came out. Adrian Urmand, who was the first to be seen in the passage, went at once to his bedroom, and then Michel descended to the little parlour. Marie was at the moment sitting on her stool of authority in the office, from whence she could hear what was said in the parlour. Satisfied with this, she did not come down from her seat. In the parlour was Madame Voss and the Curé, and George, who had seen his father from the front door, at once joined them.

'Well,' said Madame Voss, 'how is it to be?'

'I've arranged that we're to have a little picnic up the ravine to-morrow,' said Michel.

'A picnic!' said the Curé.

'I'm all for a picnic,' said George.

'A picnic!' said Madame Voss, 'and the ground as wet as a sop, and the wind from the mountains enough to cut one in two.'

'Never mind about the wind. We'll take coats and umbrellas. It's better to have some kind of an outing, and then he'll recover himself.' Marie, as she heard all this, made up her mind that if any possible store of provisions packed in hampers could bring her late lover round to equanimity, no efforts on her part should be wanting. She would pack up cold chickens and champagne bottles with the greatest pleasure, and would eat her dinner sitting on a rock, even though the wind from the mountains should cut her in two.

'And so it's all to end in a picnic,' said M. le Curé, with evident disgust.

It appeared from Michel's description of what had taken place during that very long interview that Adrian Urmand had at last become quite gentle and confidential. In what way could

173

he be let down the most easily? That was the question for the answering which these two heads were kept together in conference so long. How could it be made to appear that the betrothal had been annulled by mutual consent? At last the happy idea of a picnic occurred to Michel himself. 'I never thought about the time of the year,' he said; 'but when friends are here and we want to do our best for them, we always take them to the ravine, and have dinners on the rocks.' It had seemed to him, and as he declared to Urmand also, that if something like a jubilee could be got up before the young man's departure, it would appear as though there could not have been much disappointment.

'We shall all catch our death of cold,' said Madame Voss.

'We needn't stay long, you know,' said Michel. 'And, Marie,' said he, going into the little office in which his niece was still seated, 'Marie, mind you behave yourself.'

'O, I will, Uncle Michel,' she said. 'You shall see.'

Chapter 21

They all sat down together at supper that evening, Marie dispensing her soup as usual before she went to the table. She sat next to her uncle on one side, and below her there were vacant seats. Urmand took a chair on the left hand of Madame Voss, next to him was the Curé, and below the Curé the happy rival. It had all been arranged by Marie herself, with the greatest care. Urmand seemed to have got over the worst of his trouble, and when Marie came to the table bowed to her graciously. She bowed in return, and then eat her soup in silence. Michel Voss overdid his part a little by too much talking, but his wife restored the balance by her prudence. George told them how strong the French party was at Colmar, and explained that the Germans had not a leg to stand upon as far as general opinion went. Before the supper was over, Adrian Urmand was talking glibly enough; and it really seemed as though the terrible misfortunes of the Lion d'Or would arrange themselves comfortably after all. When supper was done, the father, son, and the discarded lover smoked their pipes together amicably in the billiard room. There was not a word said then by either of them in connection with Marie Bromar.

On the next morning the sun was bright, and the air was as warm as it ever is in October. The day, perhaps, might not have been selected for an out-of-doors party had there been no special reason for such an arrangement; but seeing how strong a reason existed, even Madame Voss acknowledged that the morning was favourable. While those pipes of peace were being smoked over night, Marie had been preparing the hampers. On the next morning nobody except Marie herself was very early. It was intended that the day should be got through at any rate with a pretence of pleasure, and they were all to be as idle, and genteel, and agreeable as possible. It had been settled that they should start at twelve. The drive, unfortunately, would not consume much more than half an hour. Then what with unpacking, climbing about the rocks, and throwing stones down into the river, they would get through the time till two. At two they would eat their dinner - with all their shawls and greatcoats around them - then smoke their cigars, and come back when they found it impossible to drag out the day any longer. Marie was not to talk to George, and was to be specially courteous to M. Urmand. The two old ladies accompanied them, as did also M. le Curé Gondin. The programme for the day did not seem to be very delightful; but it appeared to Michel Voss that in this way, better than in any other, could some little halo be thrown over the parting hours of poor Adrian Urmand.

Everything went as well as could have been anticipated. They managed to delay their departure till nearly half-past twelve, and were so lost in wonder at the quantity of water running down the fall in the ravine, that there had hardly been any heaviness of time when they seated themselves on the rocks at half-past two.

'Now for the business of the day,' said Michel, as, standing up, he plunged a knife and fork into a large pie which he had placed on a boulder before him. 'Marie has got no soup for us here, so we must begin with the solids at once.' Soon after that one cork might have been heard to fly, and then another, and no stranger looking on would have believed how dreadful had been the enmity existing on the previous day - or, indeed, how great a cause for enmity there had been. Michel himself was very hilarious. If he could only obliterate in any way the evil which he had certainly inflicted on that unfortunate young man! 'Urmand, my friend, another glass of wine. George, fill our friend Urmand's glass; not so quickly, George, not so quickly; you give him nothing but the froth. Adrian Urmand, your very good health. May you always be a happy and successful man!' So saying, Michel Voss drained his own tumbler.

Urmand, at the moment, was seated in a niche among the rocks, in which a cushion out of the carriage had been placed for his special accommodation. Indeed, every comfort and luxury had been showered upon his head to compensate him for his lost bride. This was the third time that he had been by name invited to drink his wine, and three times he had obeyed.

Now, feeling himself to be summoned in a very peculiar way - feeling also, perhaps, that that which might have made others drunk had made him bold, he extricated himself from his niche, and stood upon his legs among the rocks. He stood upon his legs among the rocks, and with a graceful movement of his arm, waved the glass above his head.

'We are delighted to have you here among us, my friend,' said Michel Voss, who also, perhaps, had been made bold. Madame Voss, who was close to her husband, pulled him by the sleeve. Then he seated himself, but Adrian Urmand was left standing among them.

'My friend,' said he, 'and you, Madame Voss particularly, I feel particularly obliged to you for this charming entertainment.' Then the innkeeper cheered his guest, whereupon Madame Voss pulled her husband's sleeve harder than before. 'I am, indeed,' continued Urmand. 'The best thing will be,' said he, 'to make a clean breast of it at once. You all know why I came here, - and you all know how I'm going back.' At this moment his voice faltered a little, and he almost sobbed. Both the old ladies immediately put their handkerchiefs to their eyes. Marie blushed and turned away her face on to her uncle's shoulder. Madame Voss remained immovable. She dreaded greatly any symptoms of that courage which follows the flying of corks. In truth, however, she had nothing now to fear. 'Of course, I feel it a little,' continued Adrian Urmand. 'That is only natural. I suppose it was a mistake; but it has been rather trying to me. But I am ready to forget and forgive, and that is all I've got to say.' This speech, which astonished them all exceedingly, remained unanswered for some few moments, during which Urmand had sunk back into his niche. Michel Voss was not ready-witted enough to reply to his guest at the moment, and George was aware that it would not be fitting for him, the triumphant lover, to make any reply. He could hardly have spoken without showing his triumph. During this short interval no one said a word, and Urmand endeavoured to assume a look of gloomy dignity.

But at last Michel Voss got upon his legs, his wife giving him various twitches on the sleeve as he did so. 'I never was so much affected in my life,' said he, 'and upon my word I think that our excellent friend Adrian Urmand has behaved as well in a trying difficulty as, - as, - as any man ever did. I needn't say much about it, for we all know what it was. And we all know that young women will be young women, and that they are very hard to manage.' 'Don't, Uncle Michel' said Marie in a whisper. But Michel was too bold to attend either to whisperings or pullings of the sleeve, and went on with his speech. 'There has been a slight mistake, but I hope sincerely that everything has now been made right. Here is our friend Adrian Urmand's health, and I am quite sure that we all hope that he may get an excellent, beautiful young wife, with a good dowry, and that before long.' Then he too sat down, and all the ladies drank to the health and future fortunes of M. Adrian Urmand.

Upon the whole the rejected lover liked it. At any rate it was better so than being alone and moody and despised of all people. He would know now how to get away from Granpere without having to plan a surreptitious escape. Of course he had come out intending to be miserable, to be known as an ill-used man who had been treated with an amount of cruelty surpassing all that had ever been told of in love histories. To be depressed by the weight of the ill-usage which he had borne was a part of the play which he had to act. But the play when acted after this fashion had in it something of pleasing excitement, and he felt assured that he was exhibiting dignity in very adverse circumstances. George Voss was probably thinking ill of the young man all the while; but every one else there conceived that M. Urmand bore himself well under most trying circumstances. After the banquet was over Marie expressed herself so much touched as almost to incur the jealousy of her more fortunate lover. When the speeches were finished the men made themselves happy with their cigars and wine till Madame Voss declared that she was already half-dead with the cold and damp, and then they all returned to the inn in excellent spirits. That which had made so bold both Michel and his guest had not been allowed to have any more extended or more deleterious effect.

On the next morning M. Urmand returned home to Basle, taking the public conveyance as far as Remiremont. Everybody was up to see him off, and Marie herself gave him his cup of coffee at parting. It was pretty to see the mingled grace and shame with which the little ceremony was performed. She hardly said a word; indeed what word she did say was heard by no one; but she crossed her hands on her breast, and the gravest smile came over her face, and she turned her eyes down to the ground, and if any one ever begged pardon without a word spoken, Marie Bromar then asked Adrian Urmand to pardon her the evil she had wrought upon him. 'O, yes; - of course,' he said. 'It's all right. It's all right.' Then she gave him her hand, and said good-bye, and ran away up into her room. Though she had got rid of one lover, not a word had yet been said as to her uncle's acceptance of that other lover on her behalf; nor had any words more tender been spoken between her and George than those with which the reader has been made acquainted.

'And now,' said George, as soon as the diligence had started out of the yard.

'Well; - and what now?' asked the father.

'I must be off to Colmar next.'

'Not to-day, George.'

'Yes; to-day; - or this evening at least. But I must settle something first. What do you say, father?' Michel Voss stood for a while with his hands in his pockets and his head turned away. 'You know what I mean, father.'

'O yes; I know what you mean.'

'I don't suppose you'll say anything against it now.'

'It wouldn't be any good, I suppose, if I did,' said Michel, crossing over the courtyard to the other part of the establishment. He gave no farther permission than this, but George thought that so much was sufficient.

George did return to Colmar that evening, being in all matters of business a man accurate and resolute; but he did not go till he had been thoroughly scolded for his misconduct by Marie Bromar. 'It was your fault,' said Marie. 'Your fault from beginning to end.'

'It shall be if you say so,' answered George; 'but I can't say that I see it.'

'If a person goes away for more than twelve months and never sends a word or a message or a sign, what is a person to think, George?' He could only promise her that he would never leave her again even for a month.

How they were married in November, and how Madame Paragon was brought over to Granpere with infinite trouble, and how the household linen got itself marked at last, with a V instead of a U, the reader can understand without the narration of farther details.

Printed in Great Britain
by Amazon